Father Forgive Me

and other stories

Compiled by

David Allan Hamilton

DeeBee

FATHER FORGIVE ME AND OTHER STORIES

For information contact:
David Allan Hamilton:
david@writeyourfirstnovelnow.com

ISBN: 9781896794631

First Edition: June 2022

10 9 8 7 6 5 4 3 2 1

Contents

FATHER FORGIVE ME

Amy M. Paronto

FATHER CARLO, AS HE DID NEARLY EVERY NIGHT AT eight o'clock, climbed into his car, a vehicle that could most kindly be described as a jalopy. Nicknamed the Holy Roller, it was a welcome fixture on the streets of a parish characterized by poverty and crime. Anyone who needed a ride could get one simply by flagging Father Carlo down as he cruised the streets each night until midnight. He made exceptions only for illness and Mass on Christmas Eve.

The parish benefited greatly from this service, especially Father Carlo's regulars—latchkey teens who hung out at the youth center, tired single mothers on their way home from the late shift at the Shop-n-Save, young men who were one bad decision away from landing themselves in jail. The Holy Roller served as a kind of mobile confessional, without the formality of sacrament or expectation of penance. It was a place to let one's guard down, where every passenger was guaranteed to find an open ear and a forgiving heart. No strings attached.

But none needed the Holy Roller more than perhaps Carlo himself. A shepherd whose flock shied from the pews was a lonely one. These days, the sheep showed up for weddings and funerals, and not much else. Every time someone got into the car and settled into the seat next to him, Father Carlo was given a chance to fulfil his calling.

On this particular night, Carlo turned onto Presstman Street to see two women at the far end of the block, one of them waving him down. He flashed his headlights in acknowledgement, and when he pulled up at the curb, he smiled at the familiar face approaching his open passenger window.

"How did you know it was me, Ms. Estelle?"

"Oh, Loretta said you was comin' this way." Estelle leaned into the window. "I got a customer for you. She new 'round here."

Carlo looked toward the woman hanging back on the sidewalk and nodded. "Hop on in."

"Go on now," said Estelle, turning to the woman. "Father Carlo run you where you need to go."

Without a word, the woman moved to the back of the car.

"You can sit up front," said Carlo. "We're not formal around here."

Heedless of the invitation, the woman opened the door and slid into the back seat with wary eyes that darted about the car, as if she were assessing it for an escape route. Carlo looked to Estelle, who gave the tiniest of shrugs.

"Everything all right with you, Ms. Estelle?"

"We doin' just fine. You take care, now, Father C."

Carlo turned to the woman in the back seat. "Ms. Estelle didn't mention your name."

Her eyes landed on his for just an instant before she looked away. "Leila," she mumbled.

"Nice to meet you, Leila. Where can I take you?"

She hesitated to give him even this critical piece of information. "You know where Mountjoy Road is?"

"Sure." Carlo tried to conceal his surprise. Mountjoy Road was practically in Groverton.

"Head there," she said. "I'll tell you when we get close."

Her anxious demeanor was one he had seen before, and he waited a beat before saying gently, "Is everything all right, Leila?"

She gazed out the window for a few moments before answering in a soft voice. "I'm fine."

In profile, the set of her jaw was clear. Carlo could see it would be no use encouraging her to share whatever was troubling her, no matter how much it might ease her burden.

"If you're sure..."

Carlo let the question linger for a few seconds before he turned back to the steering wheel, then he pulled away from the curb and headed east for the road out of town. His attempts to engage Leila in even the most benign conversation were met with dull refusal. He let her be, occasionally glancing at her in the rearview mirror.

She finally spoke again only as he turned onto Mountjoy Road. "You can drop me at the edge of the woods."

"Here?" Carlo said. The nearest house was easily a quarter of a mile away. "It's dark, let me take you all the way."

"This is it." Her voice was firm. "Stop here."

Carlo frowned with concern. "Let me walk you, then. See that you get home safely." He was by no means a superstitious man, but local legend said these woods were haunted.

"Let me out, Father."

Against his better judgement he stopped, every nerve in his body on edge. Leila got out of the car in one fluid motion and the door slammed shut.

"Leila — "

She whirled to lean into the passenger window. "What would you do, Father?" Her eyes flashed sharply. "What would you do if you were asked to do something terrible, but you knew that in the end it was the right thing to do?"

Gooseflesh prickled his arms as her eyes bored into his. A sudden burst of wind rustled the leaves on the trees.

"What would you do, Father?"

Shaken by the intensity of her words, Carlo could only watch as she disappeared into the woods.

* * *

HER QUESTION NAGGED AT HIM OVER THE NEXT FEW weeks. It sat at the core of his vocation, his very being, threatening to shake his entire notion of what it meant to do the right thing. When did the ends no longer justify the means? Carlo could discern right from wrong, of course, but now he had to consider that there were degrees of rightness, to be weighed on a sliding scale. How was it possible to determine whether one thing was more right than another? Surely only God could do that. Couldn't He?

And every week he drove Leila to the edge of the woods.

They still rode mostly in silence, though the sharp edges of the wall Leila kept around her had softened into a vague unwillingness to let Father Carlo into whatever it was she kept behind it. He prayed for her, asking God to protect her from her demons, and asking Him for guidance on how to offer her comfort.

Some of Carlo's regular passengers began to talk about strange things happening near the woods. A string of foxes found dead at the west edge, with no visible explanation as to how they had perished. A freak lightning storm just outside Groverton that took out several trees along the north side of Mountjoy Road.

Tonight, when Carlo turned to greet Leila as she took her seat in the back of the Holy Roller, he was alarmed at what he saw.

"Leila, are you all right?"

She pulled her door closed. "I'm fine."

He took in the bruises covering her swollen face, the deep cut above her eye, her split and puffy lip. "You don't look fine."

"It's nothing."

"Did someone do this to you?"

She stared out the window with her mouth clamped shut. Carlo waited as long as he could.

"Leila, what happened?"

Her silence stretched on and Carlo soon saw she wasn't going to give him an answer. He turned off the ignition.

"I can't take you tonight until I know you're going to be safe there."

Leila slowly turned her head to look at him. When she finally spoke, her voice was quiet but strong. "It's only going to be worse if you get involved, Father Carlo. Let it go."

He took a deep breath. "I can't do that."

She leaned her head back against the seat and closed her

eyes. Carlo looked at her battered face and a deep shame bubbled up within him. Week after week, he had driven her to the woods, knowing something wasn't right. He should have insisted on accompanying her to wherever it was she went, hidden in the woods. He had failed her.

"Leila, what's in the woods?"

Her eyes flew open and found his. "Don't ask me, Father."

"I can't let you face this alone." He held her gaze as the question she had asked of him loomed in his mind. What would you do? He could no longer allow himself to remain ignorant of whatever trouble she was in, a sheep caught in the dark mouth of an unseen wolf, its jaws ready to snap shut and swallow her.

Finally, she said, "I don't do confession."

"This isn't a confession. Just an invitation to unburden yourself."

She searched his face as if looking for a sign that it was a trap, a trick of some kind that she couldn't trust. He let her. After a time, she inhaled slowly and deeply, then let the air back out just as carefully as she had taken it in. She reached for the door handle and, in one sweep, was gone.

"Leila!"

The passenger door opened and Carlo's heart pounded as she settled wordlessly into the seat beside him, pulling the door closed behind her and raising the window against the chilly night air. He held his breath, afraid to break the spell of the moment with the slightest movement or sound.

They simply sat there for a minute, then two. When Leila finally began to speak, Carlo felt a shift in the close air, as though the words pouring out of her filled the car with their power, transforming it into a space as sacred as any confessional he had ever set foot in.

★ ★ ★

NEITHER OF THEM SPOKE AS HE TOOK HER TO Mountjoy Road in the dead of the witching hour. In the wake of what had passed between them, there was no need to say anything more. Carlo pulled up alongside the woods and let her out at the usual spot. For the first time, she looked at him before she exited the car.

"Thank you for the ride, Father."

She was a dozen feet from the car when he called to her. She turned.

"You have a good heart, Leila. Never lose sight of that."

The corners of her mouth pinched together in a small, tight smile. In her eyes Carlo saw the weight of the terrible burden of truth she carried, shared now between them. "Yes, Father."

She dissolved into the darkness of the woods, and Carlo could not bring himself to drive away. A transformation had taken place, for both of them, and he was unprepared for how it affected him. He had a choice to make, a choice that could shape the course of a life. He turned off the car and, not for the first time, he leaned his forehead on the steering wheel and asked God to guide him through the next day, the next hour. Carlo wept as he had not in a very long time.

After he was spent, exhaustion overcame him, and sleep came quickly behind it.

In the greyness that preceded the sunrise, he awoke to the sound of birdsong and fingers numb with cold. He needed only a moment to orient himself, and he looked anxiously toward the woods. There was no sign of Leila, though he had expected nothing different. He rubbed his hands together for warmth, turned the key, and headed for home.

★ ★ ★

THREE DAYS LATER, ALL ANYONE COULD TALK ABOUT was the fire. The smoke could be seen from as far away as New Meadows. It took the firefighters fifty-two hours to extinguish the last of the flames.

Father Carlo drove to Mountjoy Road as soon as officials reopened it in a vain attempt to find Leila. Smoke still hung in the air and he nearly missed the turn, so unrecognizable was it without the woods rising against the sky. As soon as he saw the charred stumps, the last wisps of smoke rising from the damp ashes, he knew there was nothing to find.

The only thing he could do was pray. He prayed that she was safe. He prayed that she hadn't been the cause of the fire, and he prayed that she would turn up on Friday at their usual meeting spot. Alive.

When she didn't, he stopped praying and raced back to the woods.

It began to rain as he turned onto Mountjoy Road, big drops the windshield wipers struggled to keep up with. By the time he parked, it had become a downpour.

With the trees gone, he could see across to Groverton, the lights in its houses flickering dimly through the rain. Where the woods had been was now an eerie wasteland that sent a shiver down Carlo's spine. She was here, he could feel it. He turned up the collar of his jacket and got out of the car. Hunched against the rain, he picked his way through the blackened ruins, an unknown force pulling him toward the center of the fire-ravaged woodland.

In a clearing deep in the remains of the forest he found what he sought. Without warning, there was a flash of light brighter than a hundred suns, and in the momentary blindness that followed, Carlo saw Leila's silhouette against the glow of something so unspeakable it would haunt him until the fires of hell burned down to embers. As he bore witness to the horror before him, Leila's question seemed to rise from the ground: What would you do, Father?

Carlo felt the otherworldly aura close in on him, and as he regained his sight, he saw with perfect clarity what his answer would be. Surrounded by nothing but the ghost of the woods, he fell to his knees and pleaded to God for forgiveness.

NOBODY'S KITTEN

Margaret Woodford

I CAME UP BEHIND MAC AS HE LIT A CIGARETTE AND leaned over the deck rail. He jumped at the touch of my hand on his. "Jaysus, Olive, I thought you were going to make me walk the plank." The dark oily swell at the base of the weather-beaten pier distorted his features, twisting his lips to turn the hesitant smile into a grimace.

I took a deep breath of sea air. "Now why would I do that, Husband?"

He faced me, squinting behind a cloud of blue smoke. "Don't you blame me for losing the house?"

"Nonsense." I realised how harsh my answer sounded and tried to smile. "It's not your fault, my love. When government lackeys claim your property, and the house your poor father built with his bare hands, there's not much you can do." The words tasted caustic in my mouth, although I felt no bitterness toward Mac. "Besides..." I squeezed his hand. "I've decided to consider the bright sides."

He turned his attention to a lone dory slipping into the misty cove. "Which would be...?"

"Once they tear down the old house, sure, won't the tourists have a lovely national park?" I inhaled, thankful for the sting of the salty breeze on my face. "They can stand in my forget-me-not bed and enjoy an uninterrupted vista of the Atlantic Ocean."

"Did you say 'bright sides' plural?"

I spread my arms wide and took a turn around the deck. "What youngster wouldn't want to live on a pirate ship?"

"You mean a decrepit fishing schooner. We're just lucky Dad kept this berth."

"But to our brood, it's a pirate ship."

I could hear the relief in his laughing response. "As long as they don't mutiny." He flicked the cigarette overboard, picked up his lunch pail and brushed my lips with his. "I'm off."

"You're not getting away that easily." Unable to resist, I pressed my lips to his in a lingering kiss, then grabbed his cheek between my fingers and pinched. "Have a good day at work, Husband."

His grey eyes danced. "You're a funny duck, Missus." His laughter followed him down the gangway and rang out behind him as he strolled down the road to catch the bus. The silver lunch box flashed in the morning sunlight.

The ancient vessel creaked beneath my feet. Waves rocked the floating pier, and I gripped the handrail to descend to the galley. *Will I ever get used to this?* I wondered as I pulled on my work gloves and loaded coal chunks into the stove. *At least it's temporary.*

The deck above my head shivered, and the schooner's complaints grew with every stomp. "How do you expect my poor old boards to put up with this constant assault of tromping feet every blessed morning? I'm not getting any younger, you know."

The crew advanced on the galley.

"Good morning, my loveys." I tossed the coal-smudged gloves aside and hugged each child, the mother cat counting her kittens. Debra, Carol, Freddie, Edward and Sparky.

"Can we have dippy eggs?" Debra, the oldest, asked. She offered to set the table, but Edward and Freddie, his twin, pushed her aside.

I jumped as a handful of cutlery assaulted the solid pine. Forks, spoons, and knives crashed and scattered. "My poor nerves. Have pity." I organised the offending utensils.

I jumped to avoid the mugs and plates the twins launched into the chaos. "Have a care for Mom's nerves," one of them bellowed. "Throw over that bottle of milk." I lunged to rescue it and almost lost my grip on the glass neck, slick with condensation.

"Everyone, get out from under my feet." I plopped the bottle onto the table and shoved Edward toward the doorway. "I'll call you when it's ready."

Freddie evaded my sweeping grasp and ran across the galley, calling, "Look how my spit dances across the stove."

"You little imp. No spittin' on my stove." I dove and caught his arm, but too late. His fresh saliva sizzled across the hot surface, extracting excited giggles from the rest of them.

"Hey Ed, get a whiff of this." Freddie doubled over with laughter. "Cooked spit smells like bacon."

Edward sniffed and pinched his nose. "No, it smells like chicken," he argued. "Smatchy chicken."

"Ugh." I sniffed and decided *definitely bacon with a tinge of kippered herring. Good thing I'm not hungry.*

Unfortunately, I had to release the spitting devil to unwrap Sparky's fingers from the bread knife. She resisted, squealing, "Let me make the toast." With a jerk, I pulled the knife free, but my elbow hit a water glass. A raucous cheer arose as I spun to grab the teetering glass before it went over the edge. Frozen with my left arm around Sparky, the bread knife in my right hand and the errant glass in my left, I felt like I was posing for a bizarre photograph entitled "Domestic Efficiency."

Once I had released Sparky and the glass and stowed the knife out of reach, I picked up my broom to sweep the five of them toward the door. "Everybody out."

Debra dodged my efforts and stood with hands on hips. "We're trying to make breakfast. Get out of our galley before you break something." I had to admit, she sounded exactly like me.

With a roar, the twins tackled her to the floor. "We'll break you."

Carol, the second oldest, leaped away from the thrashing bodies. "Stop being so upstrapless, boys," she yelled.

Debra fought her way free to resume her authoritative stance. "Actually, the word you're looking for is obstreperous."

The boys continued rolling at my feet, now pummeling each other.

Carol sidestepped them. "Whatever the word is, they're being it."

"Stop it." I separated the brawling twins. "My nerves are gone."

"I'll find them." Sparky jumped on a chair. "I think they're up here." She shifted plates and cutlery aside, searching the tabletop for my lost nerves.

"Stop it," Carol ordered. "You're just shoving everything around."

Sparky stuck out her lip, then opened her mouth wide. But before the storm broke, I grabbed her and plopped her onto the floor. "For God's sake. Take her out of here. You'll have her bawlin' the once."

Debra grabbed her hand. "Come on, Sparky."

"Only Daddy's allowed to call me Sparky." She dug in her heels. "Let me go." Her high-pitched wail nailed me right behind the eyes.

"Everybody out," I yelled. "I'll call you when breakfast is ready."

"But we're hungry now." The five voices bawled in unison.

"My nerves are shot." I brought the flat of my hand down on the table, sending a tea cup rolling on its side. We all watched as it advanced in slow motion toward the edge of the table and crashed at my feet.

Wide-eyed silence ensued until, at last, they clambered up the stairs and tramped across the deck above my head.

★★

After the chaos of breakfast, I declined their offers of help and shooed them through the sitting room toward the stairs. "It's a beautiful day. Go ashore and find something to do." I stopped Debra on her way out and reminded her to keep an eye on Sparky.

The twins ignored me and circled each other with wooden swords. "We're pirates," they yelled in unison.

"I'm One-eyed Pete." Edward pulled a black patch from his pocket and stretched the elastic around his head, but before he could position it over his eye, Freddie snagged the band, snapping Edward's face. A violent dispute erupted over who would get to be One-eyed Pete.

"Actually," Carol interrupted. "All pirates wear patches and it's not because they have one eye."

Edward turned on her. "Okay, smarty pants, if they got two eyes, why do they all wear patches?"

"If you don't know, I'm not gonna tell ya." She crossed her arms and turned her back.

"Get her," Freddie roared, and they attacked, swords swinging until they backed her into the corner.

"Mom, make them stop." She raised her hands to fend them off.

"Take it outside." I dropped onto the sofa, too tired to get in the middle of it.

"Not until Miss Know-it-all tells." Freddie poked his sister in the ribs until she squealed for mercy.

"For God's sake, Carol," I begged. "Can't you just..."

"I'll tell if you give me those things." She pointed to the looming weapons.

The boys surrendered their swords and waited, bodies twitching with impatience.

"Two reasons." She held up a finger. "Reason number one—when you look through your telescope for land ho and stuff, you only use one eye."

"And what's the other reason?" Edward asked.

She placed her palm over her right eye. "Reason number B—When you come below decks, it's dark." She lifted her hand from her face, demonstrating. "You lift the patch and that one eye can see. It doesn't need to adjust or nothing. It's all very scientific."

"Give them back." With a roar, the twins attacked. Swords and bodies crashed to the deck.

I dragged myself from the sofa to separate the brawlers

and send the whole noisy brood ashore.

When the violent rocking finally stopped and the boat lay peacefully at anchor, I made tea and took my work basket to the sitting room. A cloud of dust rose as I dropped onto the settee and turned to the comfort of my knitting. The boat's rocking and the hypnotic rhythm of the needles soothed my frazzled nerves. *Peace at last.* I didn't realise I had dozed off until the sound of tramping feet shuddered the old schooner to its keel. The hatch banged, and I braced myself for the imminent attack. The raucous crew descended. Five squirming, shrill bodies poured in, filling the small space. Bright eyes and faces outshone the porthole's dim light.

Edward shouted, "Mom. We found…."

"NO, I found it." Freddie's grimy hand thrust a minikin of grey fluff into my face.

I squinted. "It's late in the year for pussy willows."

"Not pussy willows. It's a kitten."

"Mew," said the grey fluff. To me, it sounded like a plea for help.

When I reached to take the shivering ball, hand and kitten retreated. "It's mine. Please. Can I keep it?" Freddie's plea set off the rest of them.

Five bodies hit the floor, and I shielded my ears against the claims of ownership.

A plaintive "Mew" broke the cacophony. The grey fluff streaked past and disappeared beneath the bookcase. *Poor little thing,* I thought as the horde screamed.

"Mom, where did it go?" Debra asked.

I stared past the bookcase toward the porthole, trying to keep my expression noncommittal. "I didn't see."

The begging and arguing carried on with each child laying claim to the tiny creature cowering somewhere out of sight. To block out the racket, I focused on the ormulu clock sitting atop the battered wooden sea chest serving as an end table. The clock's hands travelled around its honest face. *An hour they've been at it now.*

At last, the kitten's silver head emerged, then jerked away from grasping hands. Five bodies flopped on bellies. "Come out, kitty," they bellowed.

"My kitty," Sparky screeched.

"Enough. You got me drove." I pressed my hands to my ears. "This is nobody's kitten."

"What do you mean?" Debra asked.

"I'll show you what I mean. Bring me one of Dad's work socks." To the twins I said, "Get me a hammer and nails from the toolbox."

Everyone stared open-mouthed for a split second, then the screaming and pleading began.

"A hammer and nails? A sock?"

"What are you gonna do?"

"You'll see." I crossed my arms and summoned a scowl to keep my smile at bay. "Now, stop your noise or get out."

The older girls froze while the boys huddled in the corner. Sparky knelt by the bookcase and screamed, "Don't come out, kitty. Mommy's gonna kill ya."

I hoisted her by the waist, carried her to her berth, and closed the hatch. Ignoring her indignant cries, I returned to the sitting room where I found a hammer, nails, sock, and four terrified children.

They cowered as I pointed in their direction and ordered, "Someone get a saucer of milk."

When the milk arrived, I sent them from the room. "Go ashore or to your bunks, but I don't want you here for this." Wails of protest followed as they dispersed.

I closed the door, waited for the racket to subside and set the saucer on the floor. "Here, puss," I whispered.

★ ★ ★

A MERRY CHIME FROM THE CLOCK REMINDED ME MAC would soon be home, so I sent Sparky above to pipe him aboard. As I expected, she hesitated, her lips just forming the word, "But..." I held up a finger and she obeyed, scurrying up the steps.

Moments later, Mac's heavy tread joined the light footsteps on the deck. His voice came down the hatch. "Where are the rest of the crew?" The footfalls stopped, and he added in an uneasy tone, "Why is it so quiet, Sparky?" Gentle waves rocked the schooner and its mooring lines groaned in response.

The footfalls continued, and Sparky preceded him into the sitting room.

He stood in the doorway, caught my eye, and mouthed his question. "What's happening?" He scratched his head and gazed at the remarkable scene. Carol sat in the big armchair reading *Treasure Island* to Freddie in a quiet voice while Debra and Edward splayed on the floor with a jigsaw puzzle.

The schooner swayed, sighing, echoing my gratitude as I knitted, following its rhythm. "Blessed peace."

Mac leaned against the door, wide eyed before releasing a burst of laughter. "Olive, my love. I don't know how you keep this mutinous crew under control."

I laid my knitting aside and winked. "All it takes is a firm hand on the tiller."

Sparky tugged his sleeve. "Come see, Daddy." I followed them into the galley, where the freshly scrubbed stove shared warmth and the comforting aroma of baking bread. She pointed to the rough oak wall above the table.

He stared, shook his head, and did a double take. "Why is my work sock nailed to the wall?"

I smiled. "To keep it safe. Out of reach."

"What…?"

"Pert," the sock answered. It squirmed and a small silver head emerged.

Sparky jumped up and down clapping her hands. "Can we keep the kitty?"

Mac ruffled her hair. "What does Mommy say?"

I felt three pairs of pleading eyes on me and allowed my gaze to travel the room. The kitten wriggled in her sock and said, "Mew?" *Well?*

The day's chaos replayed in my mind as I considered, remembering the sensation of the shivering creature, trusting me as I bundled her into the thick wool. "I guess every kitten needs a home."

Mac nodded. "And every ship needs a cat."

THE BATTER

Marty Wilson

DUNEDIN IS A SMALL TOWN ON THE GULF COAST halfway down Florida where you can close your eyes and gently inhale the perfume-like aroma of citrus in the air coming off the orange and grapefruit groves. The sun greets you like a warm kiss; so gentle it's almost dreamlike as you feel the heat penetrate through your skin. It's as perfect a day as you could ask for here in this welcoming little town.

There are quaint shops lining the downtown and it still holds its charm absent of the big corporate restaurants and food chains. The nearby gulf coast beaches are alive with festivals celebrating their Scottish heritage. The festivities are complete with highland dancing and a kilt-wearing bagpiper playing on nearly every corner for those that might not have known that it was Scottish week. In some kind of revelry call the bagpipe music seems to awaken the sleepy town at this time of year and Dunedin comes to life.

Every spring since 1982 a migration of managers, players, trainers and an unbelievable amount of other men and women arrive here to devote six weeks of their time and energy to spring training camp. Dunedin has been home for forty years to the Major League's sole Canadian ball team, the Toronto Blue Jays. They are the only team to stay loyal to the same spring training location all these years. The area becomes a beehive of activity as people dart from their air-conditioned cars to their air-conditioned rooms in the hopes that their pale white skin doesn't burn to a crisp.

Dunedin has a population of around thirty-six thousand Dunedites throughout the year in the off-season. However, in the springtime, it blows up to sixty thousand as people from the North flock here filling hotels, restaurants, and roadways. They come here to see the young rookies show off their budding baseball skills, as well as watch the older veterans come back for another season with the hope that their bodies can make it through another grueling year of one hundred and sixty-two regular games and thirty exhibition games. Every athlete has the same goal in common, to survive until October for what could be a shot at a divisional championship and a chance of winning the pennant.

The weather today could be described as "Garden of Eden-like." The sun is baking hot, but only dangerous to those foolish enough to let it cook their skin like peanut butter cookies left in the oven too long because grandma was too engulfed in another episode of Y&R.

This is the second Blue Jay spring training camp built in Dunedin. The first training camp quickly outgrew itself after the Jays won back-to-back championships in the 1992 and 1993 seasons. At that time, the League and the entire country took notice of this up-and-coming team. During their dominant reign players like George Brett and Alberto Alomar ruled the diamond while pitcher Dave Steib was idolized as the greatest hurler to ever pitch an inside knuckleball.

Today there is a healthy mix of young and seasoned players taking to the field. Some of the veterans are slapping each other on the back as they give each other nostalgic handshakes while chest bumping in rhythmic fashion. The younger players are acting brave and confident meanwhile just under the surface the anticipation is brimming. There is an anxious excitement in the air as the players have finally reached the culmination of all their hard work. Preparation started in childhood with their dads hitting line drives and pop flies to them in the park. They paid their dues and sacrificed through the double and triple leagues and now it's finally time to shine, and show that they have what it takes to be a Blue Jay. Unanswered questions hang heavy in the air. Will their bodies hold out? Will their natural baseball skills override their nerves?

The tough competition is not only from Canada and the USA, but athletes from the Dominican Republic who seem to have been playing the game since being weaned from their mothers as babies. They throw and catch as if the ball was an extension of their own tendons and flesh. For now, the focus is on how to make the cut from one hundred and three players and become one of the remaining twenty-six Blue Jays. Then the focus will change to devoting the next six months of their lives to not only the game, but their life-long dream.

It's the pitchers who feel the most pressure from the game. This is a group of high-strung and tense players whose divorce rates are the highest among the league. When the throwers do have solid marriages, it is because their spouses are next to sainthood and understand that in order for this to work, they have to stand behind their husbands no matter what. These women carry a large majority of their family's responsibilities, while at the same time proving to the fans and media that they have it all together.

The mound is their stage where they perform their best throws to an unfamiliar catcher while the Maui Jim's and Ray Bans sit with their clipboards behind the chain link fence and decide their fate. It's only business for these men, as they hide their mouths behind player stat sheets whispering to one another as if the pitchers could read their lips from fifty feet away. On the contrary, to many of these players, it is much more than business; it is their meaning in life to be a part of Major League Baseball.

The ballpark dust has settled and the choices have been made. The team roster has been posted in the locker room. Some of the men are letting out whoops of excitement. Others are packing their equipment as gloves are thrown angrily against locker doors. Tears turn to full blown sobbing as steam from hot showers hide an explosion of pent-up energy and disappointing feelings. Some look forward to next year's tryouts while others face a return to the farms, factories, and their town's local baseball beer leagues. Their dreams will be hung up and thoughts of what could have been will hang over them.

The team is tentatively set for this year's Toronto Blue Jays and everyone involved is exuberant. In addition to the regular roster of the main ballplayers are extra players called the "taxi squad" who will travel and practice with the team and be there to fill in for injured or absent players.

IT'S THE FIRST MORNING ON THE FIELD AND THE TEAM IS electrified. The excitement and hope is palpable. The sky is full of billowy, milk-colored clouds and the air is just cool enough to warrant light jackets. The players are feeling ready and have nothing on their minds but goals and dreams as big and lofty as the clouds above them. They all went out the night before with the coaches and trainers for a congratulatory dinner where speeches and introductions were made and the beginnings of friendships were forged.

Three weeks later in Dunedin, the team works together like a well-oiled machine. They are only two weeks away from their first exhibition game against the Baltimore Orioles. The breeze is perfect today, only noticeable enough to give an appreciation for its cooling power. A light warm up includes throws, catches, and the occasional missed pop fly. The players are all in position and ready to start the regular drills they have memorized from constant repetition.

Out from the shadows of the first base tunnel walkway, comes a stranger that none of the players have seen before. He is ruddy, tanned, and walks with authority. He is tall under his ball cap and wears a faded gray Eddie Bauer t-shirt and blue jeans. He is not wearing baseball cleats but rather just regular white kicks you would find at a local Target. He walks with confidence up to the home plate as if he owns it.

He is big, lean, and strong in the chest and his arms are naturally muscular. He unslings the Easton bat bag from his shoulder and lays it deliberately on the ground not too far from him. Pulling out three different bats, he places them on top of the bag to keep them out of the dirt. He stands up tall and erect while adjusting a headset that is covering his left ear and bends over towards the bat bag. He reaches for a bat, a Messerschmitt, hand-made out of old growth ash from northern Quebec. The bat is honed down to form a tight grain and dipped in a special blended varnish. This newcomer starts to gently run his hand up and down the bat as if the bat is alive and he is stroking a family pet. The mysterious stranger's name is Luke Tanner. He is a batting specialist.

Luke doesn't catch, run, or even interact with the other players or staff on the team. His only contact is the head coach, Tom Rice, and when he's on the field this communication is done through his headset connected to Coach Rice's Bluetooth headset on the other end. Tanner has only one job and one job only for which he is extremely well-paid for and that is to see if these baseball players have the heart and skill of a Toronto Blue Jay. He will be hitting a couple hundred balls to them over the course of the day with pinpoint accuracy.

He walks up to home plate and twists the front of his left foot into the dirt. He holds the bat in front of him, gentle but firm. His face is not set in a serious determination, but in a way that shows he is here with a job to do. He looks down at the catcher and offers a friendly nod and then turns his head out to the pitcher, looking into his eyes. The pitcher looks over to Coach Rice and shrugs his shoulders and raises his hands. The coach shouts, "You're a pitcher so pitch!"

The first pitcher to square off with Luke is Mikey Fletcher. Mikey was picked up by the Jays after he was let go by the Detroit Tigers when his contract expired last fall. The Tigers had a dismal season and wanted to change the pitching line-up so they opted not to re-sign Mikey. He is thirty-two years old and has pulled teams out of some tight pinches from time to time.

Word was passed down from the Tigers' organization that although he can execute an amazing curveball, he also has a short fuse and has been known to be ejected from games by umpires who couldn't find the humour in being cussed out by a player or having their shoes spit on. Mikey doesn't bother chalking his hands, because in his mind he truly believes that he will deliver three straight over-the-plate pitches that will put this batter to bed.

His first pitch is met with a crack and a high arc to center field, where the centerfielder did not even have to move to catch the ball. Mikey reluctantly acknowledges that this guy has some experience batting.

Next, he sends home a second ball with a spin on it. This pitch is met as easily as the first and sent out to right field. Once again, the fielder barely has to move as he catches the ball.

The third pitch isn't going to be a sleeper so the pitcher sends it low and to the inside. Against all odds, Luke cuts it sharp to left field for a perfect landing into the fielder's glove stretched high above his head. The players begin exchanging glances as the pitcher glares at the coach, but his glare is met with a whimsical smile.

The fourth pitch is hot and heavy; the hurler's pride is on the line. A fastball down and out will close the book on this batter. The pitch is met like all the others, with a line drive to a bewildered shortstop. Mikey has had enough of this and unloads an arsenal of pitches only for each to be met with well executed hits that each player catches easily as the warm up progressed.

Mikey is starting to unravel and decides to shake up the hitter by aiming a pitch at his head. The batter barely moves his head in time as the pitch comes in and makes the batter drop his hat. The next pitch comes in at his torso and just barely grazes his upper chest. The batter looks down at the catcher and in a low voice says to him, "Another throw like that and I'm going to teach the pitcher how to dance."

As the pitcher leans down, setting himself for his next

throw, he gives the batter a devilish smirk, but to his surprise the batter reaches for the top of his bag for a different bat, a Kentucky dark hickory slugger, a bat used for precision infield hits. As the pitch is released from the pitcher's masterful hand, Luke steps back to connect with the pitch and smacks it with lightning speed back to the hill where it ricochets off the mound, making the pitcher trip over his feet in an effort to get out of the way.

The next pitch is a bullet and once again, Luke drives it right at the pitcher's shins. Failing to get out of the way in time, the pitcher takes it straight on and feels the impact, causing him excruciating pain. Whether from pride or adrenaline, Mikey waves off the pitching coach who is heading towards the mound to check on him.

The final pitch sails in with a hope of doing some damage, only to be met with a reciprocating hit toward the pitcher's head, where he manages to drop to the dirt in time to save himself from a concussion. Eventually the pitcher rises to his feet, dusts himself off and walks off the mound like a scolded dog with his tail between his legs while a new pitcher comes bounding out of the bullpen.

Jim "The Flamethrower" Spencer is a Southern boy who spent his early career with the Texas Rangers. Jim is a 6'4 southpaw and when he is zoned in, he can throw the ball 105 to 110 miles per hour consistently with ease. The Jays are hoping he can be one of the starting pitchers this year if his accuracy can match his speed. He is an easy-going guy and everyone on the team likes his southern charm.

Jim's first missile is met with a line drive down to the right of the left field foul line and into the corner. Next pitch is batted to the opposite field, still just inside the foul line. The right and left fielders are having to earn their paychecks this morning.

The next pitch cracks out and everyone thinks it is going to make it 395 feet over the outfield wall, but to everyone's amazement it bounces off the top as the center fielder dives and catches it. After getting to his feet he is met with a smiling thumbs up from Luke.

The next few pitches are met with solid line drives as the players scramble to catch them. Each pitch whistles with accuracy and precision and is eagerly welcomed by Luke's Kentucky slugger. After two hours of pitching and breakneck hits, Jim is done as his arm is feeling like rubber. It is time for a new pitcher.

The next pitcher is Mark Thompsom, the youngest closing pitcher the Jays had ever had signed. He was scouted from the Florida Grapefruit league and has been groomed on the Jays' farm team in Buffalo. He grew up in Jacksonville about three hours north-west of Dunedin. At twenty-four years old, he is proving to be a remarkable thrower and what he lacks in speed and experience, he makes up for in his assortment of change-up pitches.

The coaches call him the "slice and dice" kid because they never know what he is going to be serving the batters next. Although Mark is younger, he is wise enough to recognize Luke's bat is to be respected.

Mark's first pitch is a backdoor slider and it appears to be out of the strike zone but comes back down over the plate. *Crack!* The hit is caught by the second baseman in an incredible diving catch. After that, each pitch is met with a choreographed hit and is sent to its prospective recipient as directed by the coach's orders through the headpiece that Luke is wearing.

Coach Rice now brings out the runners or, "the

cheetahs", as he likes to call them. These guys aren't typical runners but are known for their speed and ability to steal bases.

Each runner takes turns standing a few feet to the right of the home plate, and as Luke smokes each ball, they bolt for first base. These guys run like the wind and if a baseman has a chance of getting them out, they have to be quick and precise.

The Jays are expending all their energy to get a double play. The excitement is dynamic and the team melds as one throughout the practice. Perspiration and fatigue are evident, but they are matched by camaraderie and unity.

After a while, the fielders and runners are exhausted and ready for a well-deserved rest. As they stand panting, some with their hands on their hips catching their breaths and others wiping sweat from their brows, they watch Luke bend down and pick up his third bat. All eyes are on him as they try to guess what he will do next. He has proved all day that he owns each pitch that dared to come across the plate, but this last pitch was just for him, and him alone.

"The Flamethrower" releases his final pitch which is met by Luke's worn-out Louisville only to be sent to the sportscasters' booth towering somewhere around 412 feet from home plate. In their lofty booth high above the outfield, the announcers dive for cover as the ball smashes into Mickey Mantle's autographed picture on the wall and ricochets to finally land on the soundman's control panel.

After this stellar hit, Luke removes his cap to salute the team before retrieving his bats, and he walks off the field. Luke's outstanding performance leaves the team ready and confident to win the pennant.

NO STRANGER AT ALL

Kate Por

'THAT WRETCHED ALEXANDER GRAHAM BELL,' thought Jessie, 'there is never a moment's peace anymore'—but it was Jessie's ring, one long, two short, so she hauled herself up and made her way to the wall to pick up the earpiece.

"Yes, Operator."

"Jessie, it's Charles; he says it's important. One moment... *Fiona!* I can hear you breathing—this call is not for you, and you know it; it's for Jessie!" They both hear the eavesdropper's quiet click.

"Thank you for that, my friend," Jessie crooned gratefully. "Put him through."

In the fall of 1939, Charles brought his boys to St. Andrews, back to the beautiful yellow brick home in which he'd been raised. There was no work in Windsor; he had to go to the South to find a job. He said he hoped it wouldn't be for long but that Agnes was not coping with the boys. What he hadn't admitted is that he married for love and looks, but that she does not have what it takes to care for anyone, including herself. *She's too deep into the sauce again*, thought Jessie, *and my Charles just can't say a bad word about anyone.*

Jessie let out her breath. She'd worked hard her whole life, raising three children and losing two while baking for the store and running another store down on Lake Huron for the vacationers. Shrapnel took her handsome, big-hearted son John, just 25 years old, at Vimy Ridge.

All she had left of him was his blood-stained beret, some loving lace-covered postcards, a few letters where he had reassured her that he and the other boys were all right, and a war medal that did nothing to bring him home to them. Jessie knew mothers shouldn't have a favourite; what would the good Lord think of that, but if they could, it would have been John. What a waste of a life, she thought bitterly—and for what? Then not six months after the news of John, they lost Bill to the Spanish Flu despite his strapping 6'6" size and his bear-like strength. The leading hockey player in the region.

Henry, her husband, broken from losing his boys and also weakened from the flu he and Bill had both caught working the ships on Lake Huron, suffered a stroke and eventually succumbed a year later. He spent his remaining days with limited speech, staring off into the sky with his pipe in hand from the front porch or looking out the window, tears clouding his eyes.

Jessie still had Charles, her baby, now at a distance. And her three grandsons, named after their deceased uncles, Bob, William for Bill and Jamie for John. Thank the Lord they were too young to be conscripted in this new and wretched war.

* * *

THE BOYS, NOW SETTLING THEMSELVES UPSTAIRS, JESSIE turned to look at her remaining son.

"Are you ok?" she asked, seeking the truth in his eyes.

"I needed to know they'd be safe, Mum. I couldn't go otherwise."

Jessie nodded seriously; they'd be safe all right. To help Charles, she'd find it within herself to raise them alone. She took a deep breath, and asked God for strength and patience.

"Nae bother, hen. You know I'll make sure of it." Charles smiled, hearing his mother's old Gaelic expressions, taken from her grandmother, and exhaled slowly.

As their father drove away after supper, the three boys lined the porch, eyes fixed on the receding car with Jessie flanking them, her arms on two of the three shoulders.

"Get yerself off to school, William; your brothers have already left!"

William looked up from the book. "I did all my chores, and I know everything they are teaching me," he stated emphatically.

"Off with you!" she chided.

That child will be the death of me, though fondness crept in. She sat down and thought about the boys, now with her well over a year with occasional visits from their father and even less frequent ones from their mum, then she set herself to baking.

The boys clambered up the stairs yelling.

"Your trews are mocket and torn; what have you been up to, my boys, and what have you done with our William?" She leaned down to brush off Jamie's trousers.

"It's William's fault, he is constantly being weird, and we try to make him be normal," Bob's voice raced like a train, running right off its tracks.

"He won't listen to Bob," Jamie was crying, tears creating culverts down his muddy face. "And then Mrs. Black said anyone who had finished their work could do what they wanted. William stood up on his chair and started singing, and he was so loud, and it was awful! Mrs. Black said she hadn't meant that someone could sing, and the bigger ones threw things at him and laughed, and she got angry at everyone and had us sit or get the strap." Jamie's tears turned to sobs.

"At dismissal," Bob went on, his voice frightening Jessie, "they chased William, and we were yelling at him, too, telling him he always causes trouble, and then we tried to protect him, but they kicked him and said he was crazy, and that they would keep beating him until he changed and so we tried to stop them and while we were punching...."

"Where is William now?" Her voice was strained, not the controlled voice her grandsons associated with her. Images of Bill and John floated in her head, John, wounded, alone, dying, Bill, still away on the trawlers, sick and alone, both dead, gone, and she was unable to protect them or say goodbye. She inhaled sharply.

"Boys, *think*, where is William?" The boys were frightened by her tone, and Bob joined Jamie in crying now, both clinging to her by the waist.

"We don't know. He ran down the highway and wouldn't come back and then disappeared, maybe into a barn, we looked and looked, but we couldn't find him anywhere. We tried so hard, Gran, but he never answered."

"Right," she resolved, inhaling to steady her nerves and

calm her two grandsons. "But this one, I'm not losing this one. This one, this is one I will be bringing home."

★ ★ ★

FIONA KNEW SHE WAS A BUSYBODY. THIS LED HER TO moments of self-loathing, though never sufficiently to abate her curiosity. Her husband had disapproved of her eavesdropping on her neighbours' calls and used to gesture his objection strongly when he saw her pick up. However, he never dissuaded her from sharing the gossip she overheard.

Fiona knew William had disappeared. She'd overheard Jessie talking to Charles, listening to the phone call he had returned to his mother when he found out about William. He'd said William's mother refused to leave the Sandwich confectionery and wouldn't help. She knew it would take Charles too long to drive up from Arkansas to be helpful. Jessie was on her own. Usually, either Jessie or the operator caught Fiona and she'd hang up, ashamed though unable to temper her curiosity.

This time her neighbour did not sound like the woman Fiona knew so well—her voice seemed to be coming undone. The whole town knew how Jessie had lost almost her whole family in the span of 2 years, decades ago and now another one?

I'm in a real pickle, Fiona thought, as she both wanted to help but didn't want to admit to how she knew about the missing child. She decided it was best to try to find the little boy despite the unsavoury way she had come by the knowledge of his disappearance. It was, after all the Christian thing to do, she thought, parsing her logic. And he was but a wee boy.

In spite of her fear of driving, she had not done so in years, Fiona set out alone in the car. She headed down along the road where William had last been seen.

★ ★ ★

JESSIE AND HER GRANDSONS WENT DOOR TO DOOR, asking everyone if they had seen William. It had now been 24 hours, and they had talked to everyone except Fiona. The townspeople were concerned for her as she, and the car she never drove, were gone.

The word spread as far as Pine River, and confirmed that a boy in grey flannel shorts, a grey cap, glasses cocked askew, and a torn shirt had been seen jumping out of a truck.

When she stopped at the cheese factory to see if anyone had spotted the waif, Fiona discovered this herself.

"What do you mean, you gave him some cheese and sent him on his way? You did not ask him what he was doing, all alone? Weren't you concerned for his welfare? Did you not see he's but a youngster with no parents?"

Her face had reddened with anger as she'd turned on her heel, marched resolutely to the car, and shut the door. She then startled herself by pushing too hard on the accelerator pedal to create distance between her and these heathen. The wheels had screeched alarmingly; even the car emphatically disapproved of how these people had behaved. It was one thing to meddle but quite another not to help a child in need.

That boy of Jessie's must be as tough as nails to be

travelling like this all alone. He must be like his gran, who soldiered on through those dark years for Charles's sake, working as hard as can be. She had the car filled with gas, a scarce commodity those days. She decided she would continue on to Goderich and ask around there. She'd sleep at her cousin Theo's place and travel as far as need be. She couldn't tolerate the idea of a small boy alone and fearful. What could happen, dear me? What a terrible time. Fiona found her anxiety climbing as she heard of traces of his passing through. *Surely to Betsy he would manage,* she thought. H*e just had to. His Grandma can take no more.*

She relayed all her worries to her husband Theo that night, saying she would need to get up early in the morning to continue to look.

Are you mad?" He'd said. "Why you don't even know the boy, and money's mighty scarce, and here you are spending what you have left on a stranger!"

"She's my neighbour and no stranger at all, which makes it mighty important," Fiona insisted.

Theo arranged to have her travel to Windsor, with his neighbour, a cattle farmer, as he was taking some of his heifers to auction there early the next morning. Before the sun came up over the fields, Fiona had clambered into the truck gratefully. Once on the way, she opened her window a crack, "So as I feel less nauseous," she'd said, to let the smoke from his sinful smoking sweep out before it entered her lungs.\

⋆ ⋆ ⋆

JESSIE HAD USED THE TELEPHONE, NOW WITH GRATITUDE, to contact the police. A boy matching William's description had been spotted in Grand Bend, but there had been no further word. Bob and Jamie said the kindergarten to grade 8 children all sat respectfully and had never worked so hard. Mrs. Black had put the fear of God in them.

"But," Jamie had added, "everyone's normal now, so they have no one to pick on and they miss that." Bob had glared at him, but he acknowledged that life was easier without William, though they were very worried about him.

"You take care of your brothers, you hear?" Jessie had chided them. "Doesn't matter that one is a bit different; blood is thicker than water, boys, and you never again let others do as they did once he's home."

"I will swear it on the family Bible, Grandma," Bob had told her.

"I promise," Jamie had looked at her with such sad and serious eyes and her heart had swollen with love, a feeling she hadn't experienced in many years.

Once he's home, she prayed. Bring William home.

★ ★ ★

DUGAL HAD DROPPED FIONA 10 BLOCKS AWAY FROM THE address she had quickly scribbled down when looking up the shop. He said he'd meet her out front of the shop once he'd left the cattle at auction. She found the noise and dirt of the city overwhelming, and dread crept over her as she rushed across the busy streets to her destination, fearing that her mission would end badly.

Now she found herself staring at the Sandwich Confectionery, losing a little of her nerve. A bell rang as she pushed the door open, the smell of freshly baked bread greeting her, and apple pies, shelves of cans and a hot dog grill catching her eye.

"I'm looking for Agnes," she said to the young woman, whose tired face looked back at her from behind the cash register.

"She didn't come in today. I don't know where she is. She left me a note to open up alone though she left the bread and pies."

Fiona's heart sank. She sighed heavily and walked out of the store, the bells now expressing the defeat she felt so sorely. She leaned against the wall, shutting her eyes.

Voices. She heard a child's whimper and angry, loud voices.

Her eyes opened quickly, and she noticed a door to her right. She turned and knocked. The voices silenced, but no one came. This time she struck the door hard. She continued thumping it with her fist until she heard heavy footsteps on the stairs. She was surprised to see a man open the door, Scotch bottle in hand, not much older than John had been, wrapped in a woman's bathrobe.

"I am looking for Agnes."

★ ★ ★

"GRANDMA, THE TELEPHONE! CAN I ANSWER? I'VE learned my manners; I have!"

"No, Jamie," and she turned back to raise the earpiece. Jamie sat back, disappointment shadowing his face.

"Jessie, it's Fiona. She says it's urgent!"

"Oh, my. Oh, no. Oh, good, Lord. My gracious heaven." She dropped the earpiece and let out a wail and a cry of thanks. It swung to a calm still, and she held her arms open for her boys to rush in.

Later that day, Fiona pulled up beside their house in her Buick with William in tow.

Jessie had been watching from the window and ran onto the porch and down the stairs, hauling William into a great hug with his brothers cheering from above.

"Och, you're a wee Bawbag! Thank the Lord you are safe." Her eyes met Fiona's, and she mouthed, God, Bless You. Fiona nodded, got back in the car, and pulled away.

"What on earth were you thinking, William? We were worried beyond sick; I thought you would lead me straight to the grave," she asked.

"Why were you such an eejit?" Jamie cried. "Grandma's been so sad and scared, and we were afraid you'd never come home."

"Jamie, hush," Jessie admonished.

"You called him an eejit for running, Grandma! I thought you said it's what he was!"

"I dare say I had a weak moment or two, but now, we are just grateful."

"What happened, William…land's sake, your face is all black and blue!"

"Grandma, I didn't mean almost to take you to the grave because you always said to me yer a long time dead, and I don't want you dead for a long time at all. I need you."

"I am not going into the grave, boy, I promise you. Just tell us what happened."

"Well, I decided to leave because everyone was just so horrid even though I've always been told I have such a lovely voice with perfect pitch… and so I thought maybe Mum would want me now that we've been gone so long. So, I put out my thumb like we've seen others do, and first, Farmer Brown Pants picked me up and got me just past Kincardine.

Then I walked and walked till it got dark because no one wanted me. I went into a barn and slept with the sheep and the cow; she gave me a little milk." William paused

"But in the morning, I left, and Mr. Smelly Blue Suit said he'd bring me along as he was going close to Grand Bend. He thought it strange to see a boy, but I said I was grown for my age and had been working for years. And that's true, Grandma, right, we had paper routes and worked in the store, and now we do the same for you. At Grand Bend, Mr. Pipeman stopped his truck for me. He had children in the front, so he put me in the truck with his load of vegetables, and I ate a few. Don't worry, Gran, he told me I could. Then he dropped me off at the bridge in Windsor. I remembered my way home, so I walked."

William looked up soulfully at his grandmother and took a deep breath.

"I thought Mum would be happy to see me, but she was not."

"She introduced me to Uncle Tom—I didn't realize we had an Uncle Tom, I said, and she hit me hard across my cheek, angry as can be. Grandma, she and Uncle Tom didn't seem right on their feet and were sleeping in the middle of the day. So I asked if she was sick, but she yelled and said, be quiet, and told me that I'd be heading straight back to you in the morning, but not until I got a thrashing for having run away." William let out a whimper.

"You're not the one who needs a skelping, boy, though you did wrong to run."

"Then Grandma," continued William, "who would be at the door but Fiona, and she saw me at the top of the stairs. She said, "*What in tarnation?*" so loudly, and she yelled at Uncle Tom to get dressed and out of the house and hand over the hooch, and what kind of people indeed, what kind of people, she just kept saying it!

And then she saw Mum and just said, "Give me the boy, now," it was even scarier than Mrs. Black is when she's taken out the strap and had it in her hand.

I think uncle Tom was scared because before you knew it, he was dressed and shoved her against the door as he was leaving, and then Mum said I ought to go back with you and that she loved me. But she didn't seem too loving, Grandma. I didn't believe her..."

William's eyes welled up, and Jessie felt her heart squeeze hard. She hugged him. Bob patted him on the back.

Jessie remembered some of the things she had said about Fiona and regretted her impatience and irritation with the lonely woman, who had done so generously and precisely said the right things.

"Well, lad, you are loved and safe, and don't you forget it," she told him, taking his face between her hands and kissing the top of his head. "And I'll bet you are as hungry as can be. I have baked 24 Parker House Rolls, and a good many are meant for you! Take a dozen next door to Fiona and run back here for supper. Jamie and Bob run along with him and tell Fiona that there has never been a better neighbour, and should she want to join us for supper, she'd be most welcome, yes, indeed, she would."

CAN'T TELL A BOOK BY ITS COVER

Barbara Hampton

SOMETHING WHITE. WAVING AT HIM FROM UP ABOVE.

"Take a look see," he said to himself. He pulled himself up the river's bank, heavy rubber waders slipping on wet mud. Boots gaining ground now on the grass. "Nope, it's flutter in the wind. Funny didn't see it before." Something white. Hmph. Another duck left lying probably where it was bagged, he thought. A sense of nerves came over him. It grew larger the nearer he walked.

He dropped his fishing pole and ran.

The air was pristine. Damp grasses were filled with color. Stepping lightly on the tall grasses she gazed on purples, yellows, tiny whites, and then upward at chartreuse, fuchsia, soft delicate pink blossoms, and marveled that she had entered paradise. Color, colors everywhere she looked. Breathing in deeply, a sigh. Soft delicate things, no harsh oranges or clumps of red like in the desert.

Later that day she pointed to a field of dandelions on lush overgrown green and excitedly told her new friend, "Look, isn't that beautiful and oh those giant yellow bushes too," realizing that her friend was accustomed to seeing such colors and likely thought her mad. "We only had little clusters of colors and plants like that in the desert in the springtime, like on our hikes into the mountains." She wondered, am I just trying to mollify my new friend or just not make myself seem silly.

To think it was only two years ago, feeling exhausted and exasperated from cut backs and courthouses being shut down due to budget constraints. She remembered that last trip driving down the mountain pass, thinking *I'm done, I've had it.* That last hike triggered it.

Slipping her backpack over her shoulders she exited her car. Reaching inside, she found the white juniper hiking pole she'd plucked, sanded and varnished herself. After pulling it out, she slammed the door and walked into the parking lot where the group was gathering.

Slowing quickly, gazing at a newcomer. "Judge Thomas is that you?" Marilyn said.

The tall svelte figure standing up straight before her little resembled the man she'd known. No longer slouched with pouch and unkempt hair, walking like an animal of burden, the man before her was tanned and smiling. "No more judge for me," he said, "I'm retired now."

What an idea. Just to get away from it all, she thought, *now that's a plan. I can go somewhere where it's peaceful and quiet and nothing ever happens.*

This entire state is flat, she thought, *so no hiking groups except for flatlanders, and that's like taking a walk. Must buy some new clothes,* as she parked her car next to the town bookstore.

Looks inviting, she thought.

Grabbing her Gucci bag, checking herself in the mirror she touched up her lipstick, then lightly straightened her hat. Yellow jumpsuit and large sunhat sashayed into 'Jeremy's Bookshop.'

The man at the counter eyed her "My, aren't we sunny today! I'm Jeremy. I don't believe I've seen you see before," he smiled. "What can I help you locate?"

Marilyn gazed at him from under her long lashes as if contemplating a deep issue. "Is there a book club here—or anywhere in town? Because if there isn't, Jeremy, I think we should start one."

* * *

"OK FOLKS, I'M SO HAPPY TO SEE SO MANY READERS here. This is exciting. Many of you I know already. If you are new, welcome to our first meeting of the Book Clubbers. For those of you who don't know me, I recently retired from a not too exciting job in the desert of California. I moved here to be closer to greenery and where people really talk to one another. Oh, and of course, where folks love to read."

Her new friend Susan asked, "Marilyn, what's your favorite genre?"

"Who's your favorite author?" Asked another.

"Well, I'll tell you," she said, but let's hear from all of you, ok? Me? I love love love a good mystery and of course I've read and re-read Agatha many times. The best part of any mystery is figuring out who done it before the ending…if you can."

Jeremy piped up. "Did you see the recent re-make of

Death on the Nile?"

Jen jumped in with, "It was too much of a departure from the story line if you ask me."

Nodding her head, Marilyn agreed. "Yes, it did add an element, but I'm sure you were able to figure out the major twist—marry a wealthy person while you have a lover and the two of you dispose of the new spouse, right?"

Clamoring about the theft of ideas, the remaining eight joined in.

"What about that Agatha TV series," said Linda. "They did something like that there recently."

"Yeah, but did you see what they did in that other movie where the used the exact same idea…what was the name? I forget the name...," Rose said, hand to her chin where it rested most of the time she was thinking.

Sheriff John just sat for a moment, then joined in with "Yeah, but that's not real anyway—you don't see that stuff in real life. Life is more like a Lee Childs' beat-em up and killings."

The group groaned. In unison.

Chin thrust forward, Sheriff sat up. "Well let's be realistic. Not all stories have to be written in Victorian times."

"No," said Marilyn, "but the themes, same or similar themes often repeat themselves." *And a murder is a murder*, she thought.

"How's we catch a late super or just grab a drink?" Jeremy asks, pushing chairs off to the side of the room.

Marilyn starts to perk up, smiles at the invite but shakes her head. "Much as I'd love to, I'm just shot. How about a raincheck. I'd love to have a drink and chat."

Jeremy looks a bit chagrined as he locks the door. He

walks Marilyn to her car.

Wondering what it'd be like to be kissed by Jeremy, she smiles as he opens her door and says, "Let's plan on tomorrow night then, shall we?" Wondering to herself why such a pleasant man is still single, she vows to ask Susan.

Gripping the steering wheel, she manages to keep her eyes open on the drive home just as a flurry of activity streams into view. A couple flailing at one another? Probably a lover's quarrel as she flies by a silver car.

★ ★ ★

SUNLIGHT STREAMING THROUGH THE WINDOW SO *early? God why did I use the room that gets the morning sun to sleep in.*

Sluggishly moving her body, Marilyn turned to look at the clock. Fragrant aroma of coffee.

That's what I need, and someone else, some early bird up fixing it for me. Should've bought the one with a timer.

Taking a step at a time, moving steadily down the stairs she stopped at the landing. Peering out the window to make certain no early dog walkers were about, she reached for the door handle, opened and snatched the newspaper.

Ah what's this little burg up to today, she wondered. *Can't be much. Dang! Painter guy is due in an hour! Shite.*

A quick glance and she learned of a summer festival in the center of town and a woman named Kay found drowned in the creek. Coffee in hand, rushing up the stairs to dress, and the phone rings, too late to answer. The voicemail picks it up.

"Patrick here. Sorry I have to cancel our appointment for an estimate. Family emergency."

Reading through the paper, Marilyn wonders if Kay was the woman she saw along the road. Leisurely sipping her coffee, she tries to recall what the woman was wearing. Seemed more like a domestic argument. What was the color of the car? Where was this along the road? A creek? A white dress in the fog?

"Oh hell, I'm calling Susan. She'll know something."

Gazing out the window. The dwindling spring flowers. The sky began to dim and grey.

"Susan? I see I got your voicemail. Nothing major just wanted to talk about something." She then briefly relayed what she had seen along the road.

* * *

JEREMY GREETED HER WITH A SMILE AS SHE WALKED INTO his bookstore. *Maybe he knows something about this Kay who was found drowned.* He encourages her to talk about the vision as he described it, seeming more interested in the food than her story.

Shrugging her shoulders, she said, "It probably wasn't anything."

Just then the waitress dropped off the cheque. As she takes a twenty from her bag, just in case, Jeremy says, "All I have is a twenty," and places a five-dollar bill on the cheque.

Staring at the cheque, Marilyn was in shock but not the waitress standing there, as she grabbed the tray and walked off. Jeremy finished his food and sipped on his iced tea.

* * *

SOBBING, SUSAN GAVE MARILYN A HUG, UPSET OVER THE loss of her old friend. "I immediately ran over to see Patrick, her brother. You know. I wanted to offer support. He wouldn't even look up, he's so depressed and so angry. His eyes were so red like he'd been crying all night."

No wonder he didn't keep his appointment. "I hadn't realized he was her brother when I read about it in the paper. Did you mention what I'd told you over the phone?"

Wiping her eyes, Susan sits back and recalls. "I did but he says she really wasn't seeing anyone. Sheriff says it appears accidental. The creek has been rising in sections, you know."

Rising to leave, Marilyn says, "I always thought Patrick was a bit of a jerk, but I feel so bad for him right now." So tempted to ask Susan *how much of a jerk*? She thought about Jeremy in the dating department but it wasn't the moment. Susan, still wiping her eyes says goodbye.

★ ★ ★

IN A LEAP OF FAITH, MARILYN CALLS ON THE SHERIFF.

"Do you have an appointment?"

Shaking her head, she says, "I may have some information for him about the drowning."

Sheriff's clerk Terry picks up the phone and dials; she can't hear what he's saying, but then he motions her back.

"Well, hello again Marilyn. What's this I hear about information?" Sheriff John listens, thinking she's imagining things. He tells her Kay was found at a distance from the scene she 'saw' and appears to have been accidentally drowned. "There were no visible marks of a struggle on her body. And Kay was well loved around here, so don't go spreading stories."

Marilyn reminds the Sheriff that his favorite character Jack Reacher would have investigated further. Sheriff laughs. He then relays to her the only oddity is that Kay was found near the same location a drowned body had been found ten years prior.

"That was before my time," he says. "Young thing, all dressed in white like a wedding dress."

Finally, she thought, driving along the same road, *now if only I can remember the exact spot. Of course it would be raining. And hard, too.*

"Oh there—there along that slope is where I saw them arguing. Now I remember the car was silver."

Sheriff turns quickly in her direction.

"Of course, it was a sedan, I do remember now. Pull over." She jumped excitedly out of the car.

"The woman had on white; it was a blur but I remember now."

Sheriff walks toward her quietly looking around at the landscape, opening an umbrella.

"They were over in this area," as she points to the left.

Walking silently to the left, neither saying a word in a light drizzle of rain. Walking faster, ahead of the Sheriff now, a glint in the grass. Marilyn excitedly moves forward, stumbling in her heels as she tries to run toward it but falls. Sheriff comes up from behind, sees the item and pockets it as he helps her to her feet.

"Kinda slippery, running on wet grass in those heels."

⋆ ⋆ ⋆

DRIVING BACK TO THE SHERIFF'S OFFICE, MARILYN asserts, "But I know I saw something shiny lying there, didn't you see it?"

Nodding his head, he says, "Could be, and I'll go back later after I get you to your car. You're going to want to change out of those wet clothes I'm thinking." Sheriff grew silent, his thoughts now in a quandary. He recalled the Examiner's phone call early that morning.

"Although Kay appears to have been drowned and there was no blood, upon examination she'd been shot through the heart. The absence of blood was due to the arteries being cut off."

His own heart felt heavy. Instead of mentioning it, he said, "Time you bought some proper rain gear, like boots, a raincoat, and a real hat, not to mention where's *your* umbrella?"

She laughed.

* * *

THE CREEK WAS STEADILY RISING. TALK OF THE SMALL town.

"Do you suppose we'll have to evacuate at the lower end?"

Others countered, "Some already are. Hasn't been this high in some time, what with all the rain." A crack of thunder and lightning brightened the sky.

"Ah the leprechauns are at it again," Susan laughed. "They're playing ten pin, that's what my mum always said."

Marilyn was impressed and a bit edgy at the same time. She was trying to recall the last time she'd even seen rain before moving here. "This isn't just rain, it's pouring buckets!" she told Susan, thinking of boots, hats, umbrellas she didn't have.

Changing the subject, she asked, "What do you think of Jeremy, the bookshop owner?"

Susan choked on her coffee. "You must be kidding. He's dullsville and won't pick up a check not ever. That's why I was surprised he let you have the book club there but I realized he'll make money from people buying books." She shook her head. "I went out with him a couple of times and that was enough."

Gazing out the window as Susan spoke. "Oh look, there goes Patrick." She waved in his direction. A streak of silver flew by the window. "Must be in a hurry. I went out with him too, long time ago but he just never seemed interested in dating. Anyone for that matter. Hope he's careful. He's so broken up about Kay."

Susan paused, then said, "He was at Conway's, you know the florist in town. I called to order flowers for Kay's service. It'll be at Thomson's. It's the only place here. Anyway, it was so sweet. Linda said Patrick had been in and he bought two bouquets. Imagine, two he took with him. They were lilies for his and Kay's parents. He's suffering so."

She watched as water was accumulating in the street. The air crackling and the sound of thunder woke Marilyn from her thoughts. "We'd better be off, all this rain is making me nervous."

Susan laughed, but agreed the water was rising, a first in a long time. "Yep, we'd best be off while we can."

★ ★ ★

"FLOODING IS OCCURRING AT THE SOUTHERN BRANCH of the creek, and evacuation orders are now in place for Smithton to Ida. If you live in those areas or in between there is an evacuation center at the church in Maybee."

Turning off the radio, and feeling her arms tense, she pulled her shoulders down from her ears. Marilyn realized the fascination with rain was over.

This is serious, she thought. *I need to talk to someone, anyone right now.* Picking up the phone and dialing she got Susan's voicemail. *Oh heck, always a voicemail when I really need to talk.* She hung up without leaving a message.

Oh heck. She dialed again. "Susan, this is Marilyn. Wondered how you're doing in this, and why on earth are you out in it?" Big sigh. She picked up the receiver and dialed the Sheriff.

"Hi Marilyn, how are you managing. Do you need assistance? A boat to come get you?" laughed the clerk.

"Hi Terry. Funny. How you can joke in a time like this. I've never seen so much rain! Anyway, I just thought I'd check in with the Sheriff to see how he was managing what with the flooding." She could see Terry nodding his head.

"Well, there's been a serious development in a case he's working on, so he's out on it. I'll let him know you called."

★ ★ ★

WATER CAME FROM THE HEAVENS FOR DAYS, BUT IT FELT like weeks. Several homes had flooded basements. Tired of reading, Marilyn looked out the window at deep puddling. The thought of putting on her new boots and taking a walk was not appealing.

Walking to the den, she said, "Oh what the heck. See what's going on out there besides rain." Smiling, she pressed the remote. Gazing at the television screen, she shakes her head. Parts of homes were washing down the swollen creek.

She'd never seen anything quite like it. Or basements for that matter. Scenes of flooding filled the screen. A news flash appeared. The reporter was announcing that there was at least one drowning from the heavy rains. Downstream they'd found the body of a male believed to be in his fifties; floated up the embankment as the water crested. Although the reporter cautioned that he hadn't been positively identified, it was believed to be that of Patrick O'Brien, missing from the town… for several days. He'd recently lost his sister to a drowning and was despondent. Sheriff says this is being looked at as an accidental drowning and not a suicide as some have reported."

The water eventually slowed, the rain petered out to a drizzle. Boots pulled on, then off again. Umbrellas of all shapes, sizes, and colors were being shaken and put away but not too far away. Sunlight streamed broken through the clouds. Just days away from a blue sky, they said. They were fond of saying that, she observed.

Smiles again, almost like it had never happened. Back to normal whatever that was, would she ever know. Downstream a body and then a burial. Downstream white lilies were seen to float on the stream like birds fluttering in the wind taking to the waters.

THE YELLOW CARDINAL

Debbie Bhangoo

In the not-too distant future...

MADE AN APPOINTMENT WITH A TESTING LAB FOR EMBRYOS.

SPECIALIZES IN THE LATEST GENE EDITING TECH.

LET'S TALK.

CAMILLE LYON-SAIDI GRIT HER TEETH AND SHUT OFF her phone without responding to the texts. In the quiet of Chilbury Park, she unwrapped the checkered wax paper from her sandwich. Her belly growled at the sight of the Havarti, pickled eggplant, and tomato, nestled between rye.

Normal.

Camille took a bite, as she tried to untangle the splendid

mess her life insisted on being: unfinished degree after unfinished degree, down-to-nothing funds, and Seb.

Flippin' Sebastian.

Total turncoat, all of a sudden enamoured by fatherhood.

I shouldn't have told him I was late.

On the other end of the park, students zipped by with purpose, laughter spilling out of their mouths, and shining futures exuding from every stance.

Normal.

Where's my normal? Camille shook her left foot, gripping her lunch for dear life, elbows resting against her taut stomach. Pickle juice oozed down her palm, and all over her constellation ring. Damn. The one thing she treasured, and it too, couldn't escape the garbage dump trajectory of her life.

For a moment she sat, staring at her hand, accepting the state of things. Two of the three mini diamonds glinted under the soft June sun. Camille remembered them gleaming on her mom's finger, above the same wrist housing the yellow bird tattoo, and then the gems sitting alone and forgotten on her office desk, next to two cups of unfinished coffee, and a glass of whiskey.

The night Violette Lyon vanished.

"Here," a gruff voice said, startling her, and a napkin danced in front of her eyes. A man, in a beige tweed coat, with shaggy grey hair underneath a Lakers cap sat beside her, invading her perfect bubble of solitude.

"Thank you."

The man nodded. Freckles dotted his nose, and a lumberjack beard filled his face. He smelled of sesame snaps and oregano.

"Listen, this might sound strange coming out of me, but I must warn you…there's a storm coming. It might already be here."

Camille looked up at the sky, an acceptable blue, with a smattering of unthreatening clouds. She tensed. Flicked her eyes to the path leading back to the nearest building, and other people.

"There isn't much time, Camille. You're rare, unique even. You must survive what's to come. The world, humanity will need you."

Lakers knows my name.

With insides twisting, she resolved to remain calm, as she set to pack up the drying sandwich. Preposterous. Humanity had no need of her. She shot him her best deceiving smile. "I have a meeting with my TA."

He jutted out his jaw, sadness lacing his brown little eyes, hidden behind dirty glasses she only noticed now.

"Right, of course you wouldn't believe me." Tapping both his knees with his hands, Lakers frowned, and then hung his head, possibly to examine his shoes, the ground, who knew?

At last, he stood up. "If you change your mind, and want to know more, here's where to find me." He handed out a business card, blank on the upside.

"How thoughtful," she said, just to get rid of him. Camille grabbed the item, and then her world spun off its axis, plunged into the ether.

A yellow cardinal sat tattooed on the man's inner wrist.

She fought back tears. Camille wanted to erase time and nestle into the space where she last felt at home.

Mom.

Does Lakers know her? Where she took off to? *They*

have the exact same tattoo.

As a rule, Camille never trusted anyone, but when it came to her mom, all rules evaporated. If she could find purchase in her mother's orbit again, she could finally face the world. Like a normal person. Instead of sailing from port to port, forever unsatisfied. Did her mother even want to be found? Wouldn't she have already returned if she wanted to?

Camille brought her hands to her solar plexus, took a deep belly inhale. Exhaled.

It's time to properly unpack the past.

Sweat pooled in the small of her back, mouth ran dry. Camille sat up straighter. Northern Orioles flew lazily in the distance. "Do you—"

"There you are. Why didn't you respond to my texts?" Sebastian Godfrey's tall frame eclipsed Lakers, pushing the latter away. Seb looked down at him. "Can I help you?" Then as though remembering his politeness, he added, "Sir." Without waiting for a response, Sebastian turned to Camille, his grey eyes searching for ground to chain her to spot. He raised his brows. Impatient.

She shook her head. Not today. For the second time in a matter of minutes, she gathered her belongings.

Seb caught the crook of her elbow, fingers cold, despite the day sitting at the lip of summer. An odd pallor on his face. "The baby isn't just yours. You can't just get rid of it."

Clucking her tongue, she searched for patience. "It's not your decision. Don't get so attached. It's the size of a poppy seed, right now. Insignificant."

From the corner of her eye, she saw Lakers standing a few feet away. He unclasped and clasped his hands. Edgy. She needed to talk to him. Mortification bloomed on her cheeks, as she realized he most likely heard what Sebastian said. Now, a total of three people knew of the pregnancy.

Camille unhooked Seb's hand from her arm. "Let me go."

"You can't just lay to waste good Godfrey genes."

She scowled.

Seb smiled, displaying his over-white teeth. "You know the law on mandatory gene edits at the embryo stage. It's kept the likes of Huntington's disease and AIDS in their coffins." He put his arm around her shoulders. "Now, we get enhanced on top of that, depending on what parents want and can afford."

"Well your good genes have been mixed with my common one's." She shrugged him off. "Don't be a fool. Let this go."

"Violette Lyon's daughter having average genes? I don't think so."

Her mother's name stung Camille. She hated the poisonous way it came off of Seb's tongue. "What's that supposed to mean?"

He remained quiet.

She patted his neon-green t-shirted chest. "You seem to care about this poppy seed more than me." Her palm turned into a fist. She rested it on his collarbone. "You've never cared much for me. Just my last name maybe?"

"Not true."

"There are both Lyon and Saidi genes in me." Camille lowered her fingers and raised them again over her body to remind him of the obvious. Her father's Moroccan features stood out over all else. "My dad died before I was born, remember. If people didn't know better, they could say my mother adopted me."

"Yes, but—"

Both hands in fists, Camille pressed them against her thighs. "We've never been serious. This is what we agreed upon. Fun. And now the party's over."

"But the baby—"

"Since when are you so old-fashioned?" Camille huffed. She looked around Seb, but did not see Lakers. Dissolved into thin air. Disquiet spread in her chest as she tried to find him. Nothing. She cupped her chin, while tapping her right foot.

"I have a legacy to uphold. I want to ensure—"

"No, just no," Camille stated with firmness, and she walked away, palms up over her head.

Sebastian's voice droned on behind her, nevertheless. "We've to get the baby tested to make sure there's no unruly genes. This is an unconventional pregnancy. It's better to have the embryo implanted after edits. Not as we did."

She tuned him out, as noisy thoughts of her mother and her disappearance haunted her. Possessed her. Took over.

★ ★ ★

CAMILLE PLOPPED HER HANDBAG ON THE FLOOR OF HER studio apartment. The place lay dark, stuffy, smelling of lavender essential oil and remnants of the garlic from dinner last night.

Unsure of what to do, she walked to the lone window, cranked it open, and took in hungry gulps of fresh air. Camille wanted to cry, but got as far as her lips trembling before she stopped. Her cell rang, deep in the bowel of her purse. When did she turn it back on? Ignoring it, she reached into the back pocket of her jeans and pulled out the card Lakers gave her. Who even carried these nowadays? She examined the little sturdy stock paper and groaned.

Queen of Spades, nothing special. Of course. This man had no connection to her mom. Just a weirdo with a nut job calling card. Camille huffed over to the recycle bin and tossed the offending item away. Why would he know her? No one knew what happened to Violette Lyon.

Camille pushed her emotions aside, and set to cleaning her apartment. Also, an utter mess.

About an hour into the task, a knock sounded at her door. Did Lakers follow her? To Camille's disappointment, Lacey Kim from two apartments over, stood on the other side. Eyes red-rimmed. She handed Camille a key. "I have to go. Can you feed my cats while I'm away?" Her voice shook, gaze turning to the hall, as she pointed with a trembling hand. "They're taking him away."

Camille peeked out. Arun, Lacey's boyfriend, lay on a stretcher, unconscious.

"He was fine, this morning, but I don't know what happened. He got extremely sick really fast. His skin's so cold."

"Ma'am, we're going to need you to come with us to answer some questions," an EMT pulled Lacey away before she could elaborate further.

Camille set her top teeth to rest on her lower lip. "Take care," she managed, before closing the door. For a beat, she stood, fingers steepled against her mouth, wondering why she sought Lakers when the knock first sounded. At the corner of her eye, she saw the Queen of Spades staring back at her from the bin, daring her to go down the rabbit hole.

He gave her the card for a reason. Plus, the *identical* tattoo. Camille scooped it out.

Licking her lips, she brought it closer, turned it to the

right, to the left, and then upside down. Hidden on a thin line, on the Queen of Spade's dress, she saw written in fine black ink, "Peter the Roman."

She smiled. "I knew it."

Without wasting a second, Camille fired up her laptop and searched "Peter the Roman." Her screen flashed with an iMessage from Sebastian followed immediately by two others.

ANSWER MY CALL.

DON'T ABANDON YOUR KID.

YOU KNOW WHAT THAT'S LIKE.

Camille gasped and closed the alerts.

The rainbow circle swirled, as her cell jingled anew. She cursed her decrepit life. Vague memories of a spacious, bright condo, well-stocked with a fat library of books, puzzles, board games, and a hefty humming refrigerator with all of her favourite food glimmered to mind. *Why did she leave me?*

Am I my mother?

Or am I trying to avoid being her? Deserting the life early enough so it wouldn't matter?

The phone rang again, returning Camille to the completed search.

"Prophecy of the Popes," "the last pope," and a smattering of other unhelpful links displayed before her. Camille clicked on "Images." Photos of the present pope lit up the screen as well as of old books on "Peter the Roman," and "The Fall of Rome." Not a single picture of the man she met today.

A guttural growl escaped her lips as she shut off her laptop. Camille threw herself onto the futon, pulling the covers to her chin, even though a pretty summer day carried on outdoors. She didn't feel like facing the world anymore.

The yellow cardinal tattoo however, sat as a taunt in her mind. How did Lakers link-up with her mother?

A siren wailed outside. She sighed and grabbed Lacey's key.

★ ★ ★

AFTER FEEDING THE NEIGHBOUR'S TWO BRITISH Shorthairs, she noted a tablet lying on the couch with its screen on. Camille grabbed it to shut it off, but hit the volume by accident.

"*...the earth's atmosphere is changing faster than we can cope with,*" a woman from one of the open tabs elucidated.

Camille searched for the screensaver mode button.

"*More updates shortly. Moving along, another bio-terrorist apprehended, belonging to the Yellow Cardinals Group.*"

The hairs on her arm rose. Heart raced.

"*Freja Pedersen was arrested on the outskirts of Aalborg this morning.*"

Fingers shaking, she rifled through the tabs until she found the right one.

A tall red-head in hand-cuffs, book-ended by two cops appeared on screen. The camera zeroed-in on her wrist.

Camille gasped.

Another yellow cardinal tattoo.

★ ★ ★

BACK AT HER PLACE, SHE FIRST GOOGLED "YELLOW cardinal," while realising she needed to find Lakers straightaway, and also wondering if her mother might be a bio-terrorist.

The search spewed out: "Extremely rare yellow cardinal spotted," and "...are considered a one-in-a-million sighting. The yellow coloring is believed to be caused by a genetic mutation."

Camille bit her lower lip. *Lakers called me rare.* She shivered, and then the mounting storm within unleashed at last. Her entire body trembled. Unable to take it, Camille walked away from the laptop as far as possible. She paced back and forth, hands pulling at her hair. No. no. no. no. *I can do this.* With an exaggerated sigh, Camille returned to the search and did something she hadn't done in ages.

Googled her mother.

Violette Lyon's pretty face smiled from a photo where she donned a lab coat, a sensible mute lipstick, and a blunt bob cut.

A tear fell, skimming Camille's cheekbone, then landing on her hand, as she scrolled.

She did not unearth anything new. Everything Google threw at her, she already knew.

"Violette Lyon, a famed biochemist who went corporate and helped create designer babies through germline gene editing, but then disappeared, deleting all of her data, beforehand."

Not a single mention about bio-terrorism. Camille tapped a thumb on the keypad. She set her fingers down to search for Violette Lyon and the Yellow Cardinals Group when a grimy old photo caught her eye. Her mother, in a laboratory, along with some of her associates. One of them glared back at her through beady brown eyes and a red bushy beard. A younger version of Lakers. Camille scrolled for a name and found one: Pieter Romanus.

Immediately, she googled "Pieter Romanus" but no current address came up. In fact, no new updates since the time he worked with her mother.

Strange.

His possible associate just got arrested and her mother vanished too, maybe she ought to leave it all alone?

The cell wailed once more. It rang non-stop for several minutes, before Camille tore it out of her purse. Red with fury.

To her surprise, Veronica Godfrey's name flashed on her screen.

"Sebastian's in the hospital," his mother choked out when she answered. "Something terrible is happening. Check the news."

Camille turned on the TV, ice sliding into her veins. She ended things with Seb, but she never wanted anything bad to happen to him.

"Listen dear, he told me about the baby...," but Camille no longer heard Veronica's voice. Four people knew now. Too far, Seb, too far. She hung up the phone, without a further beat. His family will take care of him. Camille turned her focus to the news reporter.

"*...a shocking turn of events, babies who have since had germline genome edits, as per global safety guidelines, are now unable to survive the new changes happening in the planet's atmosphere. The danger is equal to any of their descendants. The edits performed to eradicate harmful diseases in humans...*"

She gasped. *What? That's everyone.* She turned the volume up.

"*The heads of nations are looking into calling a world-wide emergency, but first they must meet to discuss...*"

Another siren shrieked somewhere outdoors.

"*They were not designed for these changes the planet is experiencing, and their bodies didn't know to evolve to accommodate them. People are starting to get sick.*" A ruddy man, perhaps a scientist, commented. "*The edits got rid of the diseases, but surely got rid of other factors we didn't fully comprehend before. Two sides to one coin, you know. This is what we get for playing God.*"

"*So, are you saying it would have been best to leave humans, edit free?*" The newscaster asked.

Camille heard no further. Violette Lyon got touted as a crusader in germline gene editing. Of course, she must be designed to be the baby her mother wanted. Her heart stopped. Cold. Fear snaked within Camille, and she dashed to the window and shut it in hopes of keeping the treacherous earth atmosphere out. Pointless, she knew. Camille wrapped her arms around her body, quaking.

What now?

What's the point in anything?

She had barely lived.

Camille grabbed her purse and headed out to get a drink. *The baby and I are going to die anyway.*

* * *

A HAND COVERED THE RIM OF HER GLASS OF GLENLIVET, breaking her study of its amber depths. The scent of sesame snaps and oregano wafted over.

Pieter Romanus.

"I wouldn't do that if I were you," he muttered, counteracting the loud din of the bar.

Camille laughed at the irony. She spent the good part of one of her last days, looking for this man. Failed, and now he stood before her. "Who are you? Why did you give me a card that led nowhere?" she asked, unconcerned about sounding rude. "How do you even know my name?"

"Easy now. I can explain everything." His voice remained quiet. "I meant to give you another card, but gave you the wrong one. As soon as I realized my mistake, I've been trying to find you."

"Okay, I'm listening."

Pieter's eyes went from her face to checking all corners of the room "Not here, it's very dangerous for me to even be here."

"I know what those of your club have been up to." She looked to his tattoo. "My mom had one just like that. Is she—"

He shook his head, a sad, haunted look slipping over his features. "She's no more. I'm sorry."

Camille gasped, before breathlessness invaded her, and a sensation as though her heart got ripped clean out of her chest. She clutched the spot, trying to plug up the wound. Violette Lyon disappeared without a trace years ago, yet Camille kept a candle burning with bright hope, wishing she still lived somewhere on this planet, but the flame guttered out in an instant at Peter's words. A smarting throbbed behind the bridge of her nose. She closed her eyes, saving the tears for later.

"I know you, Camille, because I was there the day your mother was due to edit your genes. I've known you your whole life," Pieter continued in a rush.

He leaned over, his mouth to her ear. "Your mom never edited your genes or those of many other embryos since your birth. She began, after some time, to believe it was wise to keep some humans edit free to see what genomes evolved to come out on top. She died for it. She wasn't alone in this thinking. We are doing the important work red-tape won't allow us to do." He pulled away, looked at the tattoo and back at her. "Violette was a good and respectable person."

Camille thought about what Peter said on the bench earlier today. Mere hours ago.

"...there's a storm coming...There isn't much time Camille...You must survive what's to come. The world, humanity will need you."

She noted her palm, now, sitting against her belly, and cold seeped into her veins. She frowned. Gripped the edges of her seat with both hands.

Pieter leaned in once more and whispered, "You are unedited, making you rare, and even rarer still, because your genome rejects edits. Violette tested on her own cells and yours. You're a cure and will be a part of the new humanity, once this flare-up dies."

"So, I'm like one of the X-Men, but in reverse?'

He nodded. "Now, follow me, please."

"Are there others?"

Pieter shrugged.

"Why did you wait so long to tell me all of this?"

His eyes watered. He blinked them closed. "It's only now, that what we've done to our species is backfiring on us." He shook his head in deep displeasure. "Nature always wins."

Camille looked at her abandoned whiskey, thought about the half-sipped one years ago, and then scanned the bar. Now, the cozy atmosphere felt tainted. Everybody looked seedy. Greedy. Scary.

Her fingers touched the corner of her cell in her pocket, sirens blared on outside of the building. The world tumbling down faster and fierier than humans could contain. It finally matched how she felt every single day on the inside. Her mother no longer existed. Never coming back.

She managed a smile at Pieter, knowing Violette Lyon probably trusted him wholly, letting it settle alongside her bones. Her miraculous genes. Abnormal from the get-go. "Let me just use the restroom."

Camille got up, leaving the constellation ring sitting alongside the whiskey.

THE NULLIFER

David Allan Hamilton

KIRK BAKER DOVE BEHIND AN OVERTURNED, SHATTERED table in the seedy nightclub where he'd been waiting for his mark to appear. Phaser fire seared past him, carving a trail of scorch marks across what remained of the dingy bar. All hell broke loose when his target, a nefarious arms trader from the Debenus System, finally appeared with his tight crew of muscle and augmented women.

Baker inhaled in short breaths and peered around the table toward the main entrance. Bartok Velt had squeezed into a dark corner of the room, surrounded by his thugs with their phasers drawn.

"Velt, listen to me," The Nullifier shouted over the din. "Call off your dogs and turn yourself over to me, and we'll both walk out of here alive."

Baker waited, holding his breath.

Velt's response erupted with a flurry of phaser fire, chewing the table to pieces. Baker rolled away just as the table shattered in a mist of shards, stink and vomit.

Baker wasn't about to let a little plasma fire stop him from nabbing Bartok Velt. He set his Durkee Twelve on rapid round fire, slowed his breath, and rose.

The first thug he nailed crumpled in a mess of blood and scorched viscera. The other two, surprised at Baker's speed, tried to recover but had no chance. The Nullifier plugged one in the face, eliminating the man's head. His next shot seared through the myrmidon's torso, leaving both halves of his body in an ugly bath of gore on the nightclub floor.

The Nullifier's mission wasn't to kill Bartok Velt. Not yet at any rate. No, it was to capture him, question him about the Peak's Point incident on Tarsus, and hold him for the sector authorities. But first, he had to arrest the bastard.

Baker fired a figure 8 of plasma over the bar, but if any other thugs remained, they wanted no part of him. Velt himself had disappeared from his hole in the wall. What remained of the thick door teetered nervously on its last hinge. The Nullifier raced through the mess of corpses and gruel, kicked the door open just in time to witness Velt mount a Skyshadow racer. The arms trader sneered at him, then kicked the racer into gear, disappearing into the moonless night across the whirlwind plains.

It would be suicide to go after him without the proper equipment. Unfamiliar terrain... a cagey foe... and no back-up. Baker pocketed the Durkee in his leather holster, wiped the sweat and blood spatter from his forehead, and returned to the oppressive stench of the nightclub. He kicked at the bodies—those still in one piece—to see if any had survived.

One of the augments slumped on the floor against the side of the bar. Her circuits kept shorting, causing her head to tic sporadically to one side. Baker assessed the degree of augmentation, then squeezed the organic part of her forearm. Her eyes fixed on his. They were deep and dark, enthralling, like Lydia's.

"Tell me where he went," he said in an unrushed voice.

"I don't kn-kn-kn-know." The augment's voice pitched as she spluttered.

Baker didn't have much time. He squeezed her flesh harder. "Why is Velt here now? Of all the places to go to ground, he picked Kattaway? That doesn't add up to me."

The augment's hair tumbled across her scratched face. Whatever remained of her organics, they were clearly in shock. But the mechanized part of her kept self-diagnosing and repairing itself. When she spoke again, her voice returned to normal.

"You know nothing, Baker."

The Nullifier grew tired of this creature. Augmented or not, it required oxygen to sustain itself. It was time to turn that off. He leaned in toward the woman, thrusting his forearm into her throat and applying enough pressure to see the distress in her eyes.

"Is this how you wish to meet your creator? Covered in blood and bone on the floor of this dump?" He leaned on her more. "Well... is it?"

The augment gasped and her eyes rolled back. Her hands flailed in front of him.

"You will tell me everything."

She nodded. Baker relaxed his arm and pulled her face toward him.

"He's here... to meet Daehra Krats."

Baker frowned. "The Freedom Convoy leader?"

"Yes," she croaked. "They meet tomorrow night. Gorstam District."

"What's the trade?"

"I don't know."

"Bull. What's the meeting about? Hurry now, I don't have much time."

"Honest, I don't know. Something about scissors, I don't—"

The augment's body convulsed in a mix of organic shock and electrical current, then slumped and toppled over on its side.

The Nullifier rose to his feet and glanced around the bar one last time. If he understood the augment correctly, Velt was about to deliver a shipment of outlawed Scissor-bombs.

And that would be very bad.

In her final moments of life as she knew it, the augment's convulsions left her body partially exposed. Baker ripped a longcoat from a quivering Serpian, and covered her body with it. "Find yourself another coat, my friend. You understand?" The diminutive humanoid nodded frantically, averting his eyes.

Baker marched out of the nightclub. After his adrenaline returned to normal levels, he inhaled the cool night air and headed back to his hotel. Within moments, local authorities on racers and carriers descended on the bar. By that time, Baker had vanished into the maze of alleyways that characterized Kattaway—a funky stew of misfits, traders, rogues and flotsam who wished to remain anonymous.

He shook his head as he moved through the off-hour stragglers. Arresting Velt was his goal, but he also needed to find out where those Scissor-bombs were going, who wanted them, and why. This wasn't some shitty little deal involving farming militias and phaser rifles. The Scissor-bombs were nasty pieces of work, designed for one purpose only. He couldn't turn a blind eye to that.

Two blocks from the hotel, he glimpsed movement in the shadows beside him. The Nullifier stopped and reached for the Durkee, but someone hit him from behind with a heavy object, and stars filled his vision. He dropped to his knees and immediately felt the sting of a steel-toed boot crush his cheekbone. Everything became a blur after that. He vaguely remembered being rolled, his fingers snapped back on his firing arm, and then cold water thrown over his face. He lay on his back in the alley, staring up into the beautiful night sky.

One of the men whispered into his ear, his voice eerily high-pitched and soft. "Leave Bartok Velt alone, Mr. Baker. Or else bad things will happen to your pretty daughter." A comms device floated into his view. Lydia sat on a wooden chair, restrained by a series of binders pulled across her arms and chest. At least half a dozen myrmidons, weapons drawn, glanced between her and the camera. "When you leave Kattaway, we will release her."

★ ★ ★

BAKER HAD PULLED HIMSELF ALONG THE ROADWAY HALF the distance to the hotel before someone noticed him and helped him the rest of the way. One of the hotel cooks, in turns out. She insisted on calling a doctor but Baker wouldn't let her. The last thing he wanted now was attention.

They had Lydia.

That changed everything.

The thugs had crushed his left cheekbone, broken three of his fingers, and left deep purple contusions across his thighs and back. He set his fingers as best he could with the tools in his med-pack, froze his shattered cheek, and popped several heavy-duty painkillers down his throat. After bathing, he changed and tumbled onto the bed.

He had no choice but to abandon his pursuit of Bartok Velt. He'd forfeit his advance, of course, but he didn't play this game for the credits anyway. Lydia mused that he played it for sport, and they both laughed over that. Not sport, the Nullifier thought to himself. Not sport at all.

Sleep eluded the galactic warrior, so despite the beating those thugs had given him, he pulled on his clothes and left the hotel just as the first wisps of daylight appeared over the Conlin Hills to the east. For the first half hour, he focused on managing the pain, refusing to give in to it. Then, at the edge of a sad, grey park in the middle of filth, he stood a moment to watch the sun rise. The view stole his breath.

That's when he knew exactly what to do. And he hated himself for it.

Baker couldn't turn his back on a piece of work like Daehra Krats armed with Scissor-bombs. They're only purpose was to inflict maximum carnage and destruction. They killed mass amounts of people by unleashing micro-shrapnel that sliced through flesh and bone with equal efficiency. People died, literally, by a thousand cuts while experiencing drawn out excruciating pain. They'd been outlawed by every military unit in the Sector for that very reason. Baker had to stop the deal from going down, no matter the personal consequences. He returned to his room and slept for the rest of the day.

* * *

THE GORSTAM DISTRICT SAT LIKE A SPINELESS MASS ON the eastern edge Kattaway, its never-ending slurry of warehouses, cargo cruisers and rusted out vehicles sucked whatever soul might have once occupied it. The Nullifier gazed down on a thumbprint of poorly-lit warehouses. From his vantage point on a scarred hill beside the District, Baker had a clear view of the entire area.

Eventually, Bartok Velt arrived by racer, flanked by a pair of heavily-armed myrmidons. He grounded the vehicle, spoke to his escort, and they hauled open a warehouse door. Baker stepped gingerly down the hill, keeping to the shadows, and crept closer to Velt's position.

He recognized the guttural sound of a cargo scow long before it rattled into view. Daehra Krats hopped off the vehicle once it had grounded. She stood taller than any of the soldiers around her.

Krats was a ruthless zealot leading a disparate band of anarchists bent on overthrowing law and order in the sector for their own gain. The group's typical *modus operandi* was to protest various events, distribute fabricated stories about people being abused by those in power, and block commerce when it suited them. Since they weren't known for being excessively violent, Baker wondered what her interest was with the Scissor-bombs? Her beef centered on political leaders, not innocent people. Something had changed.

He melted into the shadows again and lowered his head. After a moment, he clenched his jaw and tightened his grip on the phaser. "Forgive me, Lydia," he whispered to himself.

Velt met Krats outside the warehouse door. Baker

couldn't hear their discussion, but after they shook hands, he knew whatever arrangement they'd made had just been concluded. With a nod of his head, Velt directed his myrmidons to haul out the crate of Scissor-bombs. Krats stopped them as they passed and inspected the goods. She grabbed one of the bombs and turned it over in her hands.

Baker held his breath. It was now, or never. He pulled a series of micro-flares from his vest pocket and launched them with a sling over the warehouse. They ignited and showered the group below with blinding light and droplets of flammable accelerant. The scene immediately burst into flame.

Soldiers shouted and assumed defensive postures around the two dealers. A pair of them fired indiscriminately into the surrounding darkness, but their vision remained impaired. Baker cat-pawed toward the warehouse, stopping only once to take out a handful of soldiers with phaser fire.

Krats must have regained her sight first. She drew her weapon and knelt while Velt stumbled drunkenly around. She turned to him, taking his neck in the crook of her arm, and snapping it. The man crumpled to the ground in a heap.

Baker raced into the fiery scene, wiping out the remaining soldiers on the way. To his surprise, Krats lowered her weapon, placed a hand on her hip, and grinned. After Baker glanced around the area one final time, he approached her, weapon targeting her chest.

"I can't let you leave with these weapons, Krats," he said in a strained voice. "You understand."

Daehra Krats shrugged. "On the contrary, Mr. Baker. I will not only leave on my own accord, but you will wish me farewell and Godspeed, or whatever other expression of safe travels you feel is appropriate for the situation."

"What are you talking about?" he spat through his teeth.

Krats, holstered her weapon, retrieved the Scissor-bomb that fell from her hand during the attack, and placed it gently in the crate with the others. "Well, it's like this," she began. "You have no choice in the matter. Not really."

"Shut it, Krats. Come with me now and turn yourself in to the authorities."

She raised an eyebrow. "What, and miss all the fun? No, not a chance." She reached for something in her pocket and Baker raised the sights to his eyes. "I'm pulling out my comms device, if that's okay."

He nodded, keeping her sighted as she slowly pulled the device from her back pocket.

"I'd like to show you something." She took a step toward him.

"Stay where you are, Krats. Open your comms and toss it my way."

She punched the screen, showed it to him, and tossed it over. Baker grabbed it in one hand. Another image of Lydia appeared, still tied to a chair, surrounded by soldiers. "What the hell is this?" he demanded.

"I can't believe you're so naive, Mr. Baker. You still think Bartok Velt is responsible for kidnapping your daughter? You give him far too much credit. He's a useless piece of willow turd."

Baker struggled to see the truth, then glared at the woman. "Let her go now or so help me I'll kill you right here."

"And if you do, what then?" She brushed the hair back from her face. "You still don't get it, do you? The game has changed. We're no longer interested in social justice as you define it. We want..."

"Want what?"

Krats glared at him with hard eyes. "We want it all."

Whatever she had planned, though, was ruined with her capture. Baker approached her and grabbed a pair of cuffs from his back pocket.

"Of course you want it all. We all do. But your fun and games end now. Step away from the crate and put your hands behind your back."

"I refuse. You'll have to kill me, I suppose."

Baker gulped. He was many things, but he would not kill someone in cold blood.

"Just bear in mind that I'm not the only one involved here. You kill me, and you'll invite a world of trouble the likes of which you've never seen." She stood tall, defiantly. "Besides, you'll never see your daughter again. But perhaps that's not as much of a consideration as we imagined." She placed her hands behind her back and turned. "Cuff me if you wish, Mr. Baker. But understand that a long line of others is right behind me."

Baker snapped. His vision turned black with rage and he lunged toward her. With a ferocious swipe, he felled her with one blow. But she remained conscious, and chuckled.

"You think you can intimidate me? Don't you see?" Krats struggled to her knees before him. "I'm replaceable. Can you say the same for your cherished Lydia?"

Baker moved faster than he'd ever moved before. For a moment, shock registered in Krats' face as the man swept behind her, knocking her to the ground and kneeling on her neck.

His intention wasn't to kill her. He wanted to bring her to justice and work with the authorities to rescue Lydia. Instead, he placed more of his weight on her neck.

Krats grunted and coughed. Baker fought the urge to end her life. He had to keep her alive for questioning so he could find his daughter. But the powerful urge overwhelmed him, and he succumbed to his darkest nature.

He moved closer to her ear. "Krats, these are the last words you'll ever hear in this life."

She groaned as his knee crushed her larynx.

"Daehra Krats," he whispered. "Consider yourself nullified." He released the full breadth of his weight on her neck and remained there until her face turned blue and her breath ceased.

Baker stood and wiped his forehead with his sleeve. In the distance, echoes of sirens floated over the night air. The Nullifier pulled a chunk of timer-plastic from his vest, set the countdown for 60 seconds, and tossed it into the crate of Scissor-bombs.

He raced toward the hills, searching for protection of any kind. He found an old ditch and dove into it just as the crate of death exploded, brightening the night sky and casting razor-like shards around him. Baker wrapped his arms around his head and pressed into the side of the ditch for protection.

In a moment, the deadly rain ceased and the full magnitude of what he'd just done crushed him. He knelt in the dirt, fighting back tears of guilt and shame, wondering if he'd now sentenced Lydia to death.

Perhaps he had.

He rose, inhaling deeply, gazing into the night sky, and paused.

Then again, perhaps he hadn't.

He squared his jaw, grabbed his weapon, and bolted into the darkness.

SOPHIA IN G MINOR

Julia Moss

WHENEVER BACH'S PRELUDE IN G MINOR COMES ON, I am transported to that time we were at the lake house in November. The cottagers have all left and the days stretch out into lengthening nights and grey spindle trees longing for their greenery. That was the season when Sophia, my wife, would gaze out at the lake long since abandoned by the ducks and loons and listen to me play. She would hold me there in her suspended love, suspended of thought and memory and even of emotion. We beheld each other in the peace of the spheres of sound when all else was quiet.

Now, they want me to decide what we will do with her body. Will we bury her body, and in what state, or will we cremate it and spread the ashes, or place them here, in this barren bit of earth abandoned in the fields? Where will we memorialize my Love, my wife, and Sacha's mother? Surely not here, not where her mother was buried, the one-time plan. This place is all but forgotten. Moss creeps up the granite of other markers bleached by sunlight and parched by earth so dry that the dust forgot. Like the bones that lie within the earth, within the box that has no right to be a box, no right to its varnish and beauty now that her beauty is gone. This is not where she should be.

Gone for good, they say, you know that expression. What is gone for good, but hawkish neighbours and leftovers that were too dry to begin with? Like the fields no longer fit for growing. Like my Sophia who lies buried in the dirt, her bones returning to dust, and me with my memory as powdery as the rest of it.

Only J.S. brings me back. Oh, Sophia would smirk if she heard me say that, but I escape into the houses of our happiness as often as I can. They say the mind favours those memories which make us the most content. We tend to sort out and forget the hard times making them easier, and the easier times making them glisten and glow with a sparkle that may never have been there. I don't care, because if this is all I have left of her I want it to just sparkle—in memory of her.

The sun hits the adjacent marker now with an especially harsh midday light. The peach granite is nearly white, much like her skin became at the end. So quickly, the fading, all of a sudden when life turns away in exhale. A twig snaps behind me, and I turn, startled, but relieved to see Sacha. He's come after all. I'd hoped in his eyes I'd met a touch of sympathy and camaraderie through which we might connect ever so briefly. Sophia kept us together in life, and now in her death the question sitting unspoken between us is whether there will be any more Christmases or birthday dinners. I nod.

"Dad." He stops short of touching my arm.

I keep my eyes trained on Sophia's mother's name, etched into the stone. "Who could have chosen the name Edna?"

"Agreed. Hideous name. How are you, Dad?" Sacha

rubbed some dust off his shoe onto the back of his pant leg. He gestured to the plot at our feet. "So? What do you think?"

I waited for his fidgeting to stop. It was constant motion with him, always the constant motion. From a little boy it had seemed to me my son was born without the ability to appreciate a beat. No silent pauses with Sacha, ever—just a constant rushing.

I removed my jacket. The tweed was neat and precise and it soothed me to touch it, to press it into flat edges end to end and drape them over my arm. I pulled it tight and looked at Sacha's nose. Slightly upturned, like hers. "Well?" I asked him.

"I said, do you like the site? For mom's stone? And what about the ashes?"

I found a handkerchief in my jacket pocket that Sophia had put there once. "S'pose it'll do, for the stone. Like I said: I'm not sure I want to have her cremated."

I could hear Sacha scratching his scalp, rubbing his ear. He was working up to saying something he thought I didn't want to hear. It was telegraphed by the hitch of his breath.

"You know her wishes were clear, Dad."

He said the word like he thought it should soften the blow. My chest tightened in a spasm, followed by a pain over my right eye that revealed itself as tears. Whenever I brought my mind to consider the word—cremation—I was repulsed. The horror of flames, the sounds of a crematorium. Who could choose that? Who could—my lovely Sophia, with her silver waves and steel-blue eyes, her eyebrows flashing wit and examination—

The breeze blew a dried leaf our way and it brushed my cheek. I liked the way it looked: defined and fragile in this state of disintegrating back into nature.

"It doesn't seem natural, Sacha."

We kept looking at the patch of dried grass and scraggly weeds. After a while, we shuffled back to our vehicles, Sacha droning on about a wine course he was taking.

When he quieted, his hand was on the frame of the car door and he stood there, looking at me.

"What's that?"

"I said, do you want to come over for dinner with Kelly and me?"

Stunned, I promised to be there at seven.

We said our goodbyes while I crouched into the front seat. I pressed play on the car stereo. *The Magnificat* crept through the speakers at me. I had forgotten it the CD in there since Christmas. The arrangement was so sublimely triumphant and delicate, perfect for The Virgin. It brought me peace. I backed away from the cemetery, my being suspended once more in the sounds of genius. Every natural thing swayed in its place as I drove away from the cemetery and into the city, each element shimmering firmly in its place while the cosmos declared the Glory of Creation as only a tenor can do.

Later that evening, sharing an unexpected meal with my son and his wife, I surprised myself by launching suddenly into an unusual topic for us. "You know, the Israelites believed that a body had to be buried whole and intact." I dissected a chicken bone at the dining table in their meticulously impersonal home.

"Pardon?" said Kelly.

"The Israelites. The Tribes of Jacob. They believed that a body had to be buried whole and with all of its pieces, otherwise the body might not be resurrected. Tail bone, I think it was" The tender meat yielded as my tongue delighted in the sauce. My fingers were a mess. Why chicken wings?

Sacha did not directly reply. "Can we turn off the bloody harpsichord?"

"What's wrong with the harpsichord? It's irritatingly hard to play, you know."

"It's irritating, pure and simple. And I don't think it was only a Jewish tradition, Dad. How about some Chopin? Nice and neutral."

Kelly stood. "Let me choose some lighter music and then we can continue our meal. Anyone ready for more wine?" Kelly busied herself with the wine and music, but Sacha was distracted.

He rushed in. "Are you saying you've suddenly found a fondness for Jewish death rituals? Is this why you won't let Mom be cremated?"

"Really, Sacha!" Kelly gave him some more greens and filled his cup with a sparkly white. "Do you know, I had the nicest conversation today with Mrs. Belloughby from across the street. She came over with a casserole, bless her heart."

"Bill."

"What's that?"

"It's Billoughby."

"Sacha, your Mother and I had many conversations about her wishes, not just the one that you happened to hear. You shouldn't assume she was so settled on cremation. Actually I think it was the idea of you and me together on the lake to spread—!"

Sacha cut in. "Her final conversation in the hospital room, spoken through tubes and groans of pain? It was hardly a mere musing on her *options*."

My knife clattered to my plate.

I stared at him them mumbled something. It felt like my ribcage was tearing inward, slicing through my heart. I groped my way away from the table to the bathroom and closed the door. A buzzing filled my ears until it receded into a high-pitched whine that left me breathless. I fumbled at the cold water tap and tried to recall the melody line I'd heard later that day.

With effort, the Piano Concerto in D Minor ran through my memory, its faint pulsing of bass notes urging me to breathe. I imagined Sophia's fingers floating across the keys, her wrists rotating over the trills, her elbows as still as her eyes, soft and misting in both surrender and suppleness. I could almost recall her scent.

I imagined her raising her eyes to mine. Their directness pierced my heart.

When I returned to the dining room it had been cleared. Sacha and Kelly were talking softly in the kitchen, cleaning up.

"All right then," I called in my clearest voice. "I'll be on my way!" I picked up my tweed jacket and hat and was closing the door behind me before Sacha could wish me goodnight. I caught sight of a tea towel but turned my head and waved, not wanting to see the emotion in his eyes, to feel it condemning me. Sophia's gaze was enough.

That night was like a visitation. I fell asleep quickly enough, but what must have been a couple of hours later I was awakened in a cold sweat, feeling like ice was pricking my skin. Beyond my eyelids I detected a bluish haze, so I resisted opening my eyes. I squinted them tight against the light and what knowledge it might bring.

There was a presence with the cold and the light—that I

know for certain. How? As sure as you know when someone is staring at you from across a room or an auditorium, I was certain that if I opened my eyes I would see Sophia's form and it terrified the hell out of me. I drew the blankets up over my head, hoping that if I refused to acknowledge her that she would go away; well, that the ghost of her would go away. If I'd thought it was really my Sophia then it would have been the fulfillment of all my dreams. But that just wouldn't be natural.

I tossed and turned the rest of the night, unable to relax enough to settle into a regular sleep cycle. Eventually at about four AM I gave up trying and went down to the kitchen to make some tea. There was something about the hour such that I suspected there was no danger of ephemeral visits.

Instead, I dug around in my library for an old cultural anthropology textbook from my teaching assistant days. It was there, the bottom of a bookshelf, tucked in amongst books on Babylonian myth and ancient archeology. Rituals related to death and dying, laid out for me in black and white, the plasticized navy blue cover curling at the edges as the seal gave way to humidity.

The sound of my thumb on the pages brought me back to my teaching days. I recalled the hope that a new textbook used to give me, infusing right through my fingertips, as if the promise of knowledge and learning was a great secret to some mysterious other universe than the ordinary one I'd inhabited. In this case, it turned out to be true, for as the pages flipped between the covers of the book I caught a flash of a familiar handwriting, albeit in a more youthful form of rounded loops and curvy lines.

There, in her own script, was Sophia's name along with

a few notes from the class. My name was on the inside page, too, along with a star and a room number. Pages were noted along the left margin with some key words circled, lines connecting concepts and pages with an underlining flourish. Two lines, in fact, highlighting page 252.

Bubbly blue ink wound rings around the paragraph describing the *Luz* bone, the ancient belief in an almond-shaped bone at the base of the spinal column that would not degrade or disintegrate with the rest of the skeleton. The *Midrash* and some biblical references referred to it as the seat of the soul and the answer to questions about how bodily resurrection was possible.

"I remember you," I breathed the words without realizing, hearing them only after they were spoken. I traced the words and lines that Sophia had used as this information captured her imagination and her sense of wonder. I remembered how bright her eyes were then, how her hair glowed like hayfields in sunshine, how her skin was as plump and fresh as ripened peach at a summer picnic.

"I'll always remember you."

When I woke a while later, I was still on the rug with the book clasped to my chest and my mouth as dry as parchment; but, my chest felt lighter, as though my lungs were fully opened again. I was relaxed.

On a whim, I brought the book over to Sacha's house. There, on the doorstep, I presented it like a newly born infant: proud and victorious. "This is how I know!"

Sacha flicked his eyes to the book and then up in the direction of my face. Perhaps they settled on my hat—certainly not my eyes. My shoulders slumped just a little.

"Know what, Dad? Please don't tell me Mom wrote her wishes in an old book."

"Well, why not? You probably don't even know which of the books in the library were hers. Your mother was very fond of anthropology, you know. She had a fascination for the rituals associated with religious and spiritual traditions.

My son was not one to roll his eyes, so it was the set of his mouth that told me his patience was running thin. There were creases at his eyes that I didn't remember seeing before, and there was a dark pallor above his cheeks.

He invited me in, where we settled in the living room with some lemonade. I reminded myself not to rush the conversation; finally, I knew instinctively that Sacha's fidgeting was not about me or our relationship.

"I had a dream last night—or something," I began. "It was as if I could feel Sophia in the room with me." I waited for Sacha's eyes to meet mine, which they did. He smiled gently.

"That's nice, Dad."

"It was uncanny! You know, I could have sworn her perfume was there, on the air. I absolutely expected that if I opened my eyes she would be looking at me in her sardonic way."

"She liked to tease you."

"You know, when I met your mother, she was at the height of her beauty and brightness. Really! She shone out from all the other students. She was like an angel, my Sophia." A bottle of Cragganmore beckoned on the bookshelf opposite. I rose to pour two glasses and handed one to my son, still waiting to hear more.

I took a sip and rolled it around my tongue, letting the fire set. "And that's to say nothing of her intellect. She was as bright and creative as she was charming and engaging. I've never met anyone like her… I could never believe that she had chosen me, can't, still, in fact. But, for all her temporal brilliance, she saw through me as if she was looking from a place of eternity."

Sacha leaned forward. "I think she was. I remember how you used to play the piano for one another at the cottage after I went to bed. Mom was special. She gave a lot to us."

Both our faces were wet. "She did."

"I can't imagine putting her into the ground."

"I can't imagine putting her into a furnace."

"I don't want her to be dead."

"Neither do I, son. Neither do I."

We came together then, on the sofa, my boy's head on my shoulder for a brief moment. I touched his hair as I'd done when he was young and he didn't want to go to bed. "What should we do?" He murmured, not moving.

"We can talk about it tomorrow."

Acknowledgement

This collection of short stories would not have been possible without the energy and enthusiasm of the Ottawa Workshop writers who contributed their talents to it. These stories emerged from the Spring 2022 workshop.

Thanks for reading! If you enjoyed this collection, please add a short review on Amazon and/or Goodreads.

Reviews mean a lot to writers, so I encourage you to support our growing writers' community by taking a few minutes now to rate this collection and write a few words of encouragement about it. And please share your copy of the book with others!

Made in the USA
Las Vegas, NV
24 July 2022

52105199R00059